GALAXY WALKERS

Kris Paulsen

GALAXY WALKERS

Written by:

Kris Paulsen

Galaxy Walkers

By Kris Paulsen

New Edition

ISBN: 979-8-9913345-0-1

Cover design by Ahmad

Illustration by Scydel Art

Published in the United States of America

Expiration date: When dragons stop hoarding tales worth telling. So… never.

For my husband. For my children. For my parents.
Thank you for your endless love and support.

You all are my inspiration
and have my whole heart.

~Chapter 1~

Lyra had been waiting to go on the sixth-grade field trip for months. If she didn't get to go, she would have to stay with the fifth graders while everyone else, including her best friend, went to the zoo.

Her parents told her she couldn't go if her grades didn't improve. She had to convince them she would do her best for the rest of the school year if they let her go.

As a last try, she asked, "Did you decide if I can go?" Her little sister once again bumped into her at the dinner table. Lyra bit her tongue, feeling the frustration build. She knew snapping at Nova would jeopardize her chances.

"Dad and I need to talk about it. We're concerned about your grades." Lyra's mom made sure everyone had a full plate of food before she joined them.

"Mom's right," her dad added.

"I'll work even harder for the rest of the year. Please, I really want to go," Lyra playfully batted her eyelashes.

"Don't push it." Her dad's stern tone was a cue to stop asking.

"Fine." Lyra couldn't hide her disappointment. She desperately wanted to go, but pushing them for an answer would inevitably end in a "no."

Nova chewed with her mouth wide open, causing little chunks to fly onto Lyra's plate. She hated sitting next to her annoying little sister at dinner. She was constantly being bumped into. Lyra thought her little sister had to be the most irritating sister in the entire world, more than any other nine-year-old.

"Mommy, I want to go to the zoo," Nova said.

"Ew! Disgusting. Don't talk with food in your mouth. And no, you can't go. It's for sixth graders only," Lyra snapped, giving her sister a sidelong glance as she shoved her plate aside. Now she'd done it. Her parents would never let her go if she couldn't control her temper.

"Yes, I can," Nova yelled at Lyra before switching to her sweet little voice. "I want to see the animals. The gorillas and polar bears and, um, the turtles."

"You'll have your chance when you're older." Lyra's mom affectionately ruffled Nova's hair.

Nova sat deep in her chair with her arms crossed tightly over her chest. Not getting what she wanted was always a tough pill for her to swallow.

"Does that mean I can go?" Lyra asked.

"No, it doesn't. No more talk of the field trip. Finish your dinner and get ready for our family walk." With his 'we-are-done-with-this-conversation voice,' her dad effectively put an end to it.

Lyra excused herself from the dinner table. She emptied her plate over the trash can, then she rinsed it and put it in the dishwasher along with her fork.

"I'll be in the garage," Lyra announced to no one in particular. In frustration, she quickly grabbed her shoes and stomped off to the garage.

Every night after dinner, the Stewarts went on a family walk. No matter how many times she'd walked the same path, Lyra was eager to see the stars light up the night sky. It was also when her over-sized dog, Hercules, was most animated. She couldn't help but smile as she watched him bounce into the garage towards her.

With Hercules' leash securely clasped to his collar, Lyra's dad opened the garage. She welcomed the refreshing cool breeze. It was an early winter night in Southern California, the only time of year that wasn't uncomfortably hot.

Lyra's light brown curly hair was blown back by the gentle wind, exposing her Pixie-shaped ears. She quickly brushed her hair forward, hoping to hide both her ears and her freckled face.

"Why don't you ever wear your hair back? I'd love to see more of your beautiful face." Her mom leaned down to kiss her forehead.

"Mom, please." Lyra felt a moment of embarrassment before Hercules pulled her forward, dragging her down the driveway.

The early winter air felt almost perfect. Warm days turned into chilly nights, revealing clear starry skies. The ambient light made it impossible to see all the stars in the Milky Way Galaxy. Lyra's attention was solely on finding a specific one.

She effortlessly recognized constellations in the night sky. During their walks, her astrophysicist mother would often talk about the universe and the constellations. Lyra knew them by heart before she could read.

She was named Lyra after the harp-like constellation. It could only be spotted in the night sky during the fall and winter months. She always searched for it when they left the house, even if she had seen it countless times. She looked for Vega, the fifth brightest star, to guide her to the Lyra constellation.

Lyra readjusted her turquoise glasses. Her mom picked out the color, insisting it would make her hazel eyes look greener. She didn't mind the color as long as she could see clearly.

Archie, her neighbor and best friend, eagerly waved to her as they rounded the corner.

"Hey, guys!" Archie jogged towards them, grinning widely. He joined Lyra, panting heavily.

"Hey, kiddo." Lyra's dad was always happy to see Archie.

"Hello, Mr. Stewart. How are you doing on this pleasant evening?" Archie asked, sounding more like an adult than a typical twelve-year-old.

"I'm good. Glad you could make the walk tonight."

"Thank you, Mr. Stewart." Archie's words were filled with genuine appreciation.

"Archie, you're an absolute charmer. You know that?" Lyra's mom laughed.

Archie smiled. "Thank you, Mrs. Stewart." Then he whispered to Lyra, "They like me better than you."

"I think they do." Lyra laughed. Lyra's mood improved when Archie joined them on their walk. Despite her having only one friend, he was her best friend, and that was all she needed.

"Now that's funny." Nova giggled.

Lyra playfully pushed her. "Go away, would ya?"

"Not a chance," Nova teased.

Lyra ignored her annoying little sister and turned to Archie. "You're extra happy tonight."

"My dad wanted to talk. Can you believe it? He actually wanted to know about my day," Archie smiled. The news filled her with joy. Deep down, she held onto hope that Archie and his dad could mend their relationship, despite the scars of the past.

"That's great, right?" Lyra asked, fidgeting with a bracelet her parents gave her on her fifth birthday. It was a clear half glass ball with the Lyra constellation inside. She hadn't taken it off since she got it. Her constant fidgeting with it was a way for her to calm her nerves.

"Yeah, I guess. I mean, it was nice to talk to him," Archie admitted, diverting his gaze towards the sky. "Find Vega yet?"

A burst of light caught her attention in the dark tapestry above. When she looked at her parents, they showed no reaction, completely unaware of what happened. It seemed like no one had noticed. A lingering sense of unease remained, even though everything looked fine. While she had observed many meteors before, this one was unlike any she had seen.

"Did you see that?" Lyra's eyes remained fixed on the sky, hoping to catch another glimpse.

"No. Was it a shooting star? Make a wish," Archie said.

Archie frequently brought up the feeling of being watched by someone, often noticing strange inconsistencies. He could sense when someone was being dishonest, almost like a human lie detector. Lyra found it strange he had sensed nothing unusual. Her awareness of her surroundings became heightened.

There was no typical trail of a shooting star. The light was excessively bright and vanished rapidly. It caused the hair on her arms to stand up like static electricity. That nobody else had noticed it troubled her. It was possible she imagined it. Despite her worries, she trusted Archie's lack of concern. She concentrated on her breathing, attempting to calm her thoughts.

The memory of her and Archie's first meeting crossed her mind. They didn't get along at first. He moved to the neighborhood the summer before fifth grade started. His grandma introduced him to her family, hoping Lyra and him, who were of the same age, would get along.

Archie's grandma told her mom about the recent loss of his mom and about how his dad's long work hours often meant that Archie spent time alone. She wanted him to make a few friends before school started. He was homeschooled by his mother since kindergarten and Archie's grandma was hoping he would have someone to hang out with during the summer.

Lyra noticed Archie's stiff and formal appearance in his perfectly pressed clothes. While admiring his perfectly polished shoes, she couldn't help but wonder why his jet-black hair was so messy amidst everything else looking flawless. She loved her hole-filled jeans, graphic t-shirts, and scribbled converse shoes she doodled on out of boredom. She remained silent, knowing they were too opposite to have anything in common. Neither did he speak as his grandma and her mom chatted.

Throughout the summer, Lyra successfully avoided Archie, but upon returning to school, she discovered Sam was bullying him on the playground.

Every day, Lyra witnessed Sam bullying other children before the bell rang, and she was becoming increasingly frustrated. Having reached her breaking point, she confronted Sam and abruptly kicked his shin with all her might. Sam lost his balance and fell, landing on his face and breaking his nose. His nose erupted in a gush of blood streaming down his face. Lyra's stomach was queasy. She hadn't meant to hurt him that badly, but when she met Archie's gaze, he gave her a grateful nod.

As they waited in the principal's office, they heard children playing on the playground. Lyra didn't care how much trouble she was in. Her perception of Archie shifted when she noticed his smile. It was a moment that marked the start of their unbreakable friendship.

Archie's voice interrupted her thoughts. "What are you thinking about?"

"Here. Take Hercules, would ya?" Lyra said, handing the leash to Nova.

With a big grin, Nova gladly took the leash. Simultaneously, her dad grasped the leash's end, preventing Hercules from pulling excessively. With Hercules leading the way, Lyra stepped aside so her mom could pass. Lyra slowed her pace, gently pulling Archie back to create distance from her family.

"What's going on?" Archie asked, his eyebrows furrowed in concern.

"Can you help me with our English assignment?"

"You know I will. Why the secrecy?"

She spoke in a hushed voice. "My parents won't let me go on the field trip if I don't get a good grade. I've been trying, but it's like the words are floating off the paper and I can't make sense of them."

"Maybe you need new glasses," Archie suggested.

Before Lyra could say anything, the street lights flickered off. She couldn't see her family. She couldn't even see Archie. The uneasiness that she had felt earlier returned, causing a chill to run down her arms once more. Lyra's hand reached out and found Archie's arm in the darkness, bringing her a sense of relief. Every muscle in his body was trembling. She tightened her grip, her breath trapped in her throat.

"Someone is here." Archie's voice quivered, "I can feel them surrounding us."

~Chapter 2~

Another burst of light suddenly illuminated the entire sky. Panicking, Lyra searched for her family. The air was electric with an unfamiliar energy.

She barely heard Nova's cries over Hercules' loud growling. She pulled Archie forward, determined to find her family.

"Mom! Dad!" Lyra cried out.

"Stay where you are. We'll come to you. Just stay still." Her father's voice seemed far away.

Her family was walking through the darkness when the soft light from her mom's cell phone partially illuminated them. Lyra's heart sank at the sight of her sister's terrified expression and her hands tightly gripping their father's leg.

Her family disappeared from sight as another burst of light blinded her. Lyra stumbled, taking Archie down with her. While attempting to stand, she was forcefully pulled away from Archie. Overwhelmed by fear, she could not scream for help.

Gasping for air, Lyra felt disoriented as panic consumed her. She closed her eyes tightly and focused on her breathing. Without warning, she was forcefully pushed into a vehicle that immediately sped off.

She regretted not fighting back. Everything seemed unreal, as if she was in a dream. She needed a plan to escape her captors. She needed to find Archie and her family.

Lyra flexed her fingers, finding her hands unbound. She questioned why the kidnappers didn't bother to secure her wrists. The realization that they didn't consider her a threat made her shudder. Before looking, she took a moment to ready herself for whatever awaited her.

"Lyra. Lyra."

Lyra's eyes flew open when she heard Archie's hushed voice. The dim light made it difficult for her to see his face clearly. Although he sat beside her, he seemed far away. It was clear he was equally terrified, as she noticed his chest rise and fall rapidly.

His eyes remained fixed in front of him while silently mouthing, "What should we do?"

Sweat coated Lyra's palms. She adjusted her position to get a clearer view of their captors. In the darkness, she could only make out the profiles of two unfamiliar men.

Surprising herself, Lyra blurted out, "Where are my parents and my sister?"

"We couldn't get to them in time. You guys are safe, and that's what matters now," the passenger replied.

"Safe?" Lyra asked, "How are we safe? You kidnapped us!"

Archie grimaced. "You are going to make them mad."

"Where are my parents and my sister?" Lyra fidgeted with her bracelet for comfort.

"The ambush took us by surprise, making it impossible to protect everyone. We could only grab you two." The driver's voice had a tinge of irritation.

"What are you talking about?" The weight of Lyra's emotions caused her voice to crack. Taking a deep breath, she held back the tears that were forming. The terrified look on her sister's face kept replaying in her mind.

"I'm confident your family is alive," the passenger said. He shifted his position in the seat to face them directly. Lyra was taken aback by the concern she saw in his eyes.

"What are you protecting us from?" Archie asked.

"We'll answer your questions when we reach the safe house." The driver said.

The passenger added, "You're our top priority. Just know that you're safe with us." He faced forward again.

"I want my family. You kidnapped us and you want us to think we're safe with you?" Lyra shouted, unable to hide her frustration.

"Listen, if we didn't save you first, you'd be dead by now. Your parents will be kept alive," the passenger said.

"Dead," Archie quietly repeated the word.

"How do you know they're alive?" Lyra asked.

"So much for waiting until we get to the house," the driver sighed. "They wanted you two, not your family. We're sure they'll keep them alive to lure you in." The wheels screeched loudly, making her cringe as the car turned onto another street.

"We have to go back for them," Lyra pleaded.

"We have someone working on recovering your family. Our orders are to keep you safe," the passenger said.

Lyra and Archie were thrown off balance when the car suddenly turned to the left.

"You've been watching us," Archie said.

The driver glanced at the passenger, but Lyra couldn't see his expression. The passenger nodded in understanding.

Archie continued, "Like I knew someone was there, but I couldn't see you."

The passenger spoke to the driver, "The boy is very intuitive."

Lyra was amazed at Archie's calmness given the seriousness of the situation. He had previously mentioned it, but she didn't grasp his meaning until now. She sensed their energy, as though it had always been a part of her surroundings.

Glancing out of the window, she caught a glimpse of blurry lights from the buildings as they whizzed by. She hadn't been focused enough on where they were going. She searched for familiar signs or names, but their speed made it impossible.

The vehicle became quieter as they entered the housing development. The driver took a few more quick turns, before turning into a driveway. The house appeared unremarkable, like many other homes in the development.

Lyra's heartbeat sped up as the garage door opened. The vehicle parked as the door came down with a thud. The sound of a metal lock clicked into place, echoing behind them. They were trapped with no escape plan.

The driver got out. "We'll explain everything inside."

With determination, she squared her body, crossed her arms, and fixed her gaze ahead. She refused to go in the house, afraid once inside she might never make it out.

Archie unfastened his seatbelt. "They're telling the truth."

The passenger asked Lyra, "What can we do to prove we're not the bad guys?"

"I refuse to willingly walk into my torture chamber," Lyra replied.

The driver leaned into the vehicle. "As much as this looks like a kidnapping, it's not. You'll have your answers, Lyra Stewart. We're running out of time before we're all in danger with no chance of rescuing your family."

"How do you know my name?" Lyra asked.

"Because we are your protectors. Please, go inside. Give us a chance to explain," the passenger said.

The driver's towered over her, narrowing his eyes. "Let me make this clear. You are in imminent danger. Saros already has your parents and your sister, Lyra. I'm sure she has Archie's dad by now. Get in the house. We need to prepare you guys to get off this planet."

Lyra knew Archie felt the truth in their words. She allowed him to gently guide her out of the vehicle and into the quiet home.

~Chapter 3~

The hallway was dimly lit, with the only light coming from a flickering bulb at the far end. Archie guided her along as they followed the driver and the passenger. Looking inside the bedrooms as they went by, she felt a sense of relief to see that they appeared tidy and ordinary.

A warm glow welcomed them as they turned the corner into a cozy living room. Archie guided Lyra to the couch. She eased herself into the comfortable cushions. Despite her awareness, she remained motionless. She struggled to comprehend the situation.

"Is she in shock?" Archie asked.

"Give her a moment. She'll be fine," the passenger said.

The interior of the house was just as ordinary as its exterior, lacking any unique characteristics. The basic brown leather couches sat in front of a large flat screen TV. Lyra's eyes scanned the room, taking in every detail as she tried to make sense of the situation.

Archie said, "What are we supposed to call you guys? You know our names, so it's only fair we know yours."

The driver's response was laced with sarcasm. "Where are our manners? We didn't properly introduce ourselves while saving your lives. Sorry, kid."

A sigh escaped from the passenger. "We have more urgent matters to discuss." He nodded towards the driver, "This is Helix. I'm Blue, like the color."

"Are those your actual names?" Archie asked, stepping closer to where Helix and Blue stood.

"Code names," Helix replied. "Want one?"

Blue rolled his eyes. "Actual names. Now, we need to get to a safe planet. It's only a galaxy away. Since you can't bend, you'll wear gluonlets and let us do the work."

"Safe planet? Bend? Gluonlets?" Lyra repeated. The words were foreign to her.

She snapped out of it, walking towards them. Near the freestanding counter-top that separated the living room from the kitchen, Helix, Blue, and Archie stood. The four sunny yellow bracelets immediately grabbed Lyra's attention. The ones she liked to wear were narrower in comparison to those. Her hand stretched out to touch it. Helix's firm grasp on her wrist brought her to a sudden stop.

"Let go of me!" Lyra insisted.

"Don't touch those," Helix snapped, releasing his grip. He maintained a close watch on her.

"What are they?" Lyra asked.

"Listen carefully." Helix's voice carried a strong sense of urgency. "We have to get you to a safe planet before Saros attacks again. We understand you have questions. Push them aside and clear your minds. Think of nothing. Once we put the gluonlets on your wrists, you will be on your way to another planet, in another galaxy. The gluonlets help in reforming your particles. Without these, you could lose a limb or possibly die."

Glancing between Lyra and Archie, Blue added, "Close your eyes, slow your breathing and imagine only a speck of light. Focus on the light the entire time. Once we arrive on the safe planet, we will remove the gluonlets. Then you can open your eyes again. Understand?"

"You said you'd answer our questions when we go in the house," Lyra pointed out. "You haven't answered any and now you want us to clear our thoughts to focus on a speck of light?"

"I know what I said, but we ran out of time. Lyra, your life depends on this. Your parents' lives, your sister's life, all our lives, including Archer's," Blue urged.

"My name is Archie," he said. Then he spoke directly to Lyra, "They are telling the truth. I can, um, feel the authenticity in their words. We should do what they say." Lyra nodded in agreement. She trusted Archie more than anyone else.

"Are you ready, Lyra?" With his hand outstretched, Blue held a gluonlet delicately between his fingertips. Helix replicated the action directed at Archie.

Despite her reservations, she resolved to go along with it. All she could do was hope they were being honest and that she wasn't going towards more danger.

Lyra gently brushed her hand against Archie's. He gave her hand a comforting squeeze before letting go. Then he extended his hand towards Helix. Following suit, Lyra held her hand out to Blue.

"Do you feel that?" Archie asked.

Lyra nodded, feeling the buzzing energy emanating from the bracelet.

"Are we teleporting to another planet?" Archie asked.

"Something like that," Blue replied. "Think of these bracelets as training wheels for traveling through the galaxies. It's called bending. Before we attach second bracelet, close your eyes, and think of a speck of light. The bracelets can only do so much, so you need to remain focused."

While facing Archie, Helix held out his other hand. Blue took position in front of Lyra and did the same. The electric sensation seemed to intensify at their connection.

Lyra closed her eyes, took a deep breath, and attempted to clear her mind. She concentrated on a speck of light. The light disappeared rapidly, and Blue's face appeared in its place. Based on his appearance, it seemed like he was in his early twenties and had a youthful look. His short, blonde hair was so pale that it looked white. It was well-tamed to the side. His hair and eyebrows created a striking contrast. The color of his eyes perfectly matched his dark brown eyebrows. She wondered why he was called Blue.

Blue's voice interrupted her thoughts. "You're not focused."

"How do you know?" Lyra asked.

"I can sense your wild energy through the gluonlets. We can't bend until your thoughts are controlled. Now, focus on the speck of light."

"You know that sounds weird, right?"

"Just do it. Picture a speck of light. Focus on it."

"What color is the light?" Lyra asked.

Blue expressed his frustration with a long, exasperated sigh.

"What? I need a color or I'll think about different colors and not be able to focus."

"Blue. Now concentrate," he ordered.

"Okay, okay. A tiny blue speck of light. Got it."

With closed eyes, she focused on a tiny blue speck of light. Instantly, an Arctic chill nipped at her skin. She was determined not to lose focus. The blue light was a bright beacon in her mind.

Blue speck of light.

Tiny. Blue. Light.

Swirling freezing air enveloped her. It coiled beneath her skin, winding through her veins. She felt sharp, prickling sensations like pins and needles. It was nearly unbearable. She lost focus. The small blue light disappeared, leaving her engulfed in an inky darkness.

~Chapter 4~

"Archer, you can't go in there. I will send for you when it's time."

Lyra couldn't identify the melodic voice that was talking to Archie.

"You can't stop me. I want to see her now," Archie demanded.

It was clear from the sharpness in his voice that he was extremely upset. She struggled to lift her heavy eyelids. She couldn't shake the feeling that something had gone terribly wrong with the bend.

"Easy there, beautiful star," the strange voice instructed.

Beautiful star? Was this person talking to her? Lyra replied, "Wa ha en u e, wr e l." Her words came out as a jumbled mess. Her heart raced with panic.

"Easy, beautiful star. Stay still. The tonic needs a few more minutes to work."

Being unable to see, talk, or move was overwhelming for her. "Wo," was the only thing she could manage. It was far from what she'd tried to say.

"My name is Nebula. I would be considered a doctor on your planet. On this planet, I am a naturopath or a healer. We don't use cell killers like your planet does. Our healing remedies are natural. It was slightly challenging to find the phosphorus you need for healing. Blue is searching for it. Once he's back, you'll be whole again," Nebula said.

"Wa!"

"No, no, no. I forget how emotional humans can be. You're going to be fine. I expect Blue back soon. In the meantime, we're having a tough time managing your friend. He's very concerned about you."

Hearing that made Lyra feel relieved. If he insisted on seeing her, then he must not have been seriously hurt. If only Blue would return with whatever she needed to heal, she could find out what happened.

The previous sensation was fading, replaced by a chilling cold that seeped into her skin. Despite being unable to move, she had a peculiar awareness of things happening within her body. She focused her body, noting any areas of discomfort or detachment. It felt like something wasn't right. She wondered why she needed phosphorus.

Thinking back to science class, she'd learned that the human body required water, minerals, and cells to function properly. She remembered that phosphorus was an essential mineral, but couldn't recall its importance to the body.

Her thoughts drifted to Archie. She pictured the intensity of his piercing blue eyes when he insisted on seeing her. The only other time she saw him like that was on picture day, when his grandma dressed him up and styled his hair. She forced him to put on jeans and a t-shirt. His reason for allowing it was solely to ensure her happiness. After his mother's death, his grandma became a constant part of his life. Since his dad was rarely home and when he was, he was working, Archie didn't really mind.

"Blue is back with the phosphorus," Nebula said. Her voice grew louder as she walked closer. "This might feel a little ticklish. Maybe like bugs crawling on your skin. There's no bugs though. Stay still and think of something that makes you happy."

Lyra concentrated on what Nebula was doing. She could feel something being slowly injected into her IV.

"Let your body relax and surrender," Nebula whispered.

Once again, a powerful feeling came crashing over her, but Lyra lacked the energy to fight it. She took a deep breath, trying to release the tension in her muscles. She wished Archie was there to hold her hand.

"Lyra, beautiful star, this will only take a few minutes. Blue said you have a younger sister and a gigantic dog," Nebula said.

Nebula's attempt to divert Lyra's attention worked. She imaged Nova, her parents, and Hercules on their nightly walk. Her mom and dad were chatting about Black Matter. She couldn't imagine herself being part of their walk. Her thoughts became hazy and elusive, almost impossible to comprehend. The image of her family was disappearing.

Her body was overwhelmed by an intense sensation. It was as though there was a wriggling mass of snakes crawling beneath her skin. She lay there, helpless and immobile. It possessed her body internally, spreading throughout. Sweat trickled down her forehead while she resisted the urge to vomit.

It vanished abruptly, leaving her feeling breathless. Inhaling sharply, she felt the cool air sting her nose. When she exhaled, the sound of a bone cracking resonated through the air. The cracking sound grew louder and more frequent. It felt like being next to a thunderous explosion, the sound vibrating through her whole body.

Out of nowhere, an excruciating pain left her breathless. It was sharp and relentless, radiating throughout her body. She realized she was screaming. When the pain subsided, she ran her hands over her body, making sure nothing was out of place. She opened her eyes, the bright light causing her to squint. Moving too quickly, she immediately regretted sitting up. She had a pounding headache and felt nauseous.

"Easy, beautiful star. Your lungs need to learn how to work again. It's been a while since they had oxygen in them." Nebula insisted that she lay down again.

Lyra took a deep breath, filling her lungs with air. She saw Nebula for the first time. Nebula had thick strands of green hair that reminded Lyra of plant stems. The light played across her skin, causing a glistening, golden glow. Nebula's appearance was so plant-like that Lyra's first thought was she must be a living, breathing plant. Nebula's almond-shaped eyes sparkled tiny, golden flecks that glimmered like stars, making Lyra feel like she was gazing into the cosmos.

"Why do my lungs need to learn how to work again? I was breathing the entire time. What happened?" Lyra's voice sounded hoarse and raspy, as though she had been yelling for hours.

"Your oxygen conservation allowed me to regenerate your bones, an excruciating process you now understand. Your body rejected the pain blockers for some unknown reason. I'm sorry."

"Growing my bones back?" Lyra whispered. She slowly sat up again, inspecting herself.

"Let me in. You can't keep her from me any longer," Archie's voice was barely audible through the thick, strange metal wall.

Lyra watched Nebula approach the wall. As she got closer, the wall split like sliding doors. She could feel Archie's anger radiate from across the room. When he saw her, his expression softened.

"She's been through a lot and needs to rest," Nebula said.

"Yeah, yeah. Got it." Archie charged forward, but Nebula swiftly blocked his path.

"Archer," Nebula warned. "She grew back most of her bones only moments ago. It was a painful process."

Archie locked eyes with Lyra. "Grew your bones back? Helix said you weren't breathing. I thought." He clenched and unclenched his fists. "I thought you. I can't lose—I—I don't understand. What happened?"

Overwhelmed by emotion, Lyra tried to hide her tears. "I'm fine now. See?" She started to get out of bed when she noticed her clothes had been replaced with a strange silky fabric.

Nebula suddenly materialized next to her. "Not yet, beautiful star. You need to rest."

"Nebula, what happened?" Archie demanded, leaving no room for negotiation.

Nebula faced Lyra. "The gluonlets malfunctioned. Blue used every ounce of energy to hold you together, but it was an impossible task for any Walker." Nebula took a deep breath and continued. "Your bones shattered, leaving you barely alive. Fortunately, your skull remained intact, shielding your brain and your ribs protected your heart. Your lungs collapsed, but somehow you conserved enough oxygen to survive. It's a skill that shouldn't have developed yet."

"You really scared us." Blue's hand felt heavy as he awkwardly patted her head. He came in so quietly that Lyra hadn't noticed until he spoke. He must have slipped in before the doors slid shut behind Archie.

The sliding door was unlike anything Lyra had seen before - a solid block of metal, with no visible handle or knob. It slid shut so tightly that it left no visible sign of being an entrance.

Archie noticed Lyra staring at the wall. "I'm as mystified as you are. This planet is unlike anything I've ever seen. They call it Alora and it's super rocky. This place, the healing pod, is partly submerged in the ground. The above ground part looks like a huge rock from the outside. Where I stayed last night was the same. They wouldn't let me stay here with you. I had to bend to the Grotto. It's like an underground castle. We have our own rooms, I mean, pods there. You have to see it."

"She's not going anywhere," Helix said. Then he spoke directly to Lyra, "You will eat and rest. You need time to heal." Then he spoke to Nebula, "Great work. You brought another back from the dead."

"Where did you come from?" Archie asked, looking towards the metal wall. "I didn't see it open again."

"Bending allows us to travel through space at the speed of thought. Light speed is technically a measure of time and is seriously slow. The brain is composed of neurons and glial cells. Neurons control conscious thoughts, while glial cells work in the background. Imagine a computer. The neurons are what you see on the screen. The glial cells are like the computer's backstage crew. When your mind is fully awakened you can manipulate every particle in your body with your thoughts," Nebula explained.

"That's how we got here, by bending. Since your minds are new to being awakened, you didn't see Helix bend. Walkers move faster than what your eyes can track. In time, your eyes will adjust," Blue added.

"Ask Blue how he got his name." Helix grinned.

"I have better questions to ask. You said we could get answers. Who are you? Why are we here? Who awakened our minds? What's a Walker? What are skills?" Archie stood with his hands on hips.

Helix's laugh echoed through the room. "That's cute, kid."

"Don't let Helix bother you. He's annoyed with me," Blue said. "We're Galaxy Walkers and your protectors. Saros has been hunting Walkers to steal their skills and make herself powerful. We brought you here to keep you hidden and train you. Saros awakened your minds without us knowing. She somehow got past us to do so. We're not sure why she left then came back, but it's clear she wants you both. She's unpredictable and dangerous," Blue explained.

"And what are skills exactly?" Archie asked.

"Skills are like both magic and superpowers," Nebula explained. "They manifest from energies that connect the mind and body to the natural world. Some skills are internal like intuition-based skills and some are external, where the energies from the natural world can be manipulated."

"That's enough for today. The girl needs her rest." Helix stood up, and simply disappeared.

Lyra's stomach let out a loud growl, reminding her that she hadn't eaten in a while. Nebula nodded in response, then disappeared just as fast as Helix did. "Will we ever get used to that? It's jarring to see someone disappear like that."

"You will in time. Nebula will be back with food, then you really should rest," Blue said. He walked over to an empty chair and let out a sigh as he sank into it.

Despite her exhaustion, Lyra's hunger continued to gnaw at her. She couldn't wait to eat something. In the meantime, she watched Archie inspect the metal wall.

"Do you think movement triggers it?" he asked.

His question was rhetorical. He often talked to himself. His fingertips traced along the wall, searching for the seam.

"It's ice cold, but smooth and solid." He bounced up and down like an excited child in front of the toy store, eagerly trying to activate the automatic doors.

Lyra giggled, "Ouch. Please stop. My insides can't handle laughing right now."

Ignoring her, Archie kept jumping around. "Why isn't it working for me? I guess I need a skill to open it." Mumbling and scratching his chin, Archie was lost in thought.

The wall suddenly parted, causing Archie to step back in surprise. Nebula walked in carrying a tray.

Lyra laughed at Archie's reaction. Her attention quickly shifted to the tray as the sweet aroma caught her interest.

"Let's get you into the chair to eat," Nebula encouraged her.

Lyra hesitated, uncertain if she could walk to the chair a few steps away. She was hungry enough to try. She stood up slowly, with Nebula by her side, and accepted her outstretched hand. The silky fabric of her gown cascaded to the floor. She paid attention to her steps as she walked towards the chair, not giving much thought to her appearance.

Her curly hair fell into her face as she cautiously stepped forward. In order to see where she was going, she pushed it back behind her ears. Despite the heaviness and lack of cooperation in her legs, she continued forward. She hoped Archie wouldn't view her as fragile. He was already aware of her difficulties in school.

"You're not fully healed yet. Slow and steady. You're doing great," Nebula encouraged. Lyra lost her balance, but Nebula quickly caught her. "You're almost there."

"She's not ready. She can eat in bed," Blue said with deep concern.

Nebula waved him off. "She knows her limits. She can stop if she needs to." She turned to Lyra. "You are stronger than you think, beautiful star."

Lyra took one last step and lowered herself onto the chair. She wished she felt strong, but her body rebelled and cried out for rest. She felt like a failure. Once more, she fought back tears and blamed herself for the failed bend. Hunger brought her back to reality, stopping the tears. Nebula adjusted the tray over her lap. Inhaling, she smelled the freshly cooked food.

"Thank you. I've never been this hungry before. Did you eat, Archie?"

"Master requested for Archie to eat with everyone in the Grotto and he'll stay in his pod there tonight. When you're better, you'll get to stay in your own pod at the Grotto, too. You will meet Master tomorrow after you've rested. Growing bones takes a lot of energy. You'll feel a little better after you eat," Nebula said. Then she spoke to Archie. "When in the presence of Master, remember to remain quiet. Only speak when spoken to. Master will not be friendly to any troublemakers. Understand?"

"I'm not a troublemaker," Archie said, offended by Nebula's comment.

"I know, but she doesn't. So, do you understand?"

"Yes, I understand," Archie said hesitantly. It served as a good reminder of their presence in a foreign world with distinct customs and ways of life.

Lyra looked at the greenish brown soup. Despite its unappetizing appearance, the aroma was tantalizing. The flavor made her mouth water instantly. It was unlike anything she had ever tasted before. She ate quickly instead of savoring the taste.

Nebula laughed, "Easy there. If you eat too fast, you'll end up with a stomachache."

Nebula's warning was too late. The soup was hearty and filling, warming Lyra's insides. Her eyes grew heavy, and she could feel her body sinking into the chair.

"Who is Master?" Lyra asked, trying to stay awake.

"She's the ruler of Alora. She's also a Walker and working on a plan to rescue your family," Blue said.

"Does she know where they are?" Lyra asked.

"We don't know where Saros is keeping them, but we will." Blue stood then. "Archie, we should join the others for dinner."

"Will I get to ask her anything? I have so many questions," Archie said.

"Not tonight. You'll need to wait until Lyra is healed. Master hates repeating herself. When you arrive, you'll meet the twins, Castor and Pollux. They will be training you guys as your skills manifest. It's time to go. Sleep well, Lyra." Blue motioned for Archie to follow.

"Are we bending there?" Archie asked.

"No, it's a short walk." He turned back to Lyra, offering her a small smile before disappearing through the doors. Archie waved goodbye before the doors sealed quietly behind them.

"Should we be afraid of this Master person?" Lyra asked.

"No, but you need to show her respect. Let's get you into bed," Nebula said, extending her arm for Lyra to take.

"It's not easy being here while Archie gets to meet everyone. None of this feels real. It's like a dream, no, a nightmare. I miss my parents and my sister. I'm so confused and have so many questions. It's strange to think that I'm on another planet." Overwhelmed with emotion, Lyra's tears poured down like rain. Leaning forward, she rested her head in her hands.

Nebula embraced Lyra tightly, pulling her out of the chair and into a warm hug. "I understand. This isn't my home planet either. I'll be right here all night. You need to rest. Tomorrow will be better." Nebula guided Lyra to the bed.

Nebula moved a tray with three small cups next to Lyra. "These tonics will have you feeling more like yourself by morning."

The bright orange cup caught her eye immediately. Lyra quickly finished the drink, but its bitterness remained. The red one was sweeter than the first. The green was last, leaving a slightly sour taste behind. She made a mental note of their colors and tastes. She was happy to be done with them.

"Why was Helix so angry at Blue?" Lyra asked, her eyelids growing heavy.

"Helix and Blue have a long history. Blue almost died during his first solo bend without the gluonlets. He looked a lot like you when you arrived here. His face, fingers and toes turned completely blue because he was without oxygen. Unlike you, he couldn't regulate his oxygen. Thankfully, the previous healer saved him somehow. Helix blames himself. He's the one who trained Blue to bend. I think seeing you like that triggered his memory from that day. He'll be fine. Helix can be prickly, but his heart is always in the right place. I have a question for you. How did you save your oxygen?" Nebula asked.

"I don't think I did anything. Maybe it was Blue?"

"He couldn't have. It's a good thing you did. It saved your life. Is your headache gone?"

"How do you know I had a headache?"

"I am a healer. I can sense these things. It's an intuition, a natural way of knowing something without being taught. Some skills are intuitive, but still need training to develop and master. Everyone has skills, but only awakened minds can fully use them. I'm glad you're already feeling the healing properties of the tonics."

Nebula cleared the tray leaving Lyra to think. Everyone had hidden skills waiting to be awakened and reach their true potential. The question of her skills lingered in her thoughts. She was overcome by fatigue before she could ask any additional questions. Satiated, she released a tired yawn.

On the brink of sleep, Lyra faintly heard Nebula's soft voice whisper, "You are more talented than you know. You will achieve great things. Your understanding of the world will never be the same. The sky is not the limit. The universe is ever expanding, making your possibilities endless. Sleep, beautiful star."

Lyra wondered who Saros was and what she wanted with her and Archie. She was excited and curious to find out what skill she'd manifest. While questions raced through her mind, she eventually fell into a deep sleep.

~Chapter 5~

The warm sunlight brushed across Lyra's face, waking her. She heard a familiar sound and felt a rush of hot air on her toes. It couldn't be what she thought it was. She quickly sat up, hoping it wasn't a dream.

"Hercules?" Her oversized puppy jumped onto the bed, causing her covers to become a tangled mess.

She couldn't tell if this was real or her imagination. They'd left Hercules on Earth so; it couldn't be real. She tried looking around to see where they were, but his big head was blocking her view. She didn't care. She closed her eyes, savoring the moment.

"Hercules!" she burst out laughing. He licked her face and kept bouncing around. "Calm down, buddy. I'm okay. I had a bad dream."

"Not a dream."

She knew that voice, but couldn't see him. She told Hercules to get off of the bed. From the opposite side of the room, Blue sat quietly in a chair. It took a moment for her eyes to adjust. She wished it was just her imagination, but she was on Alora, in the healing pod. At least, that's what she remembered them calling it.

The pod she was in didn't resemble a typical room found on Earth. The ceiling had jagged edges, while the walls were smooth and rounded. It was more of a cave than a room, but not a dark and spooky cave. It was filled with warmth and sunlight.

Reality hit her in that moment. She was on another planet. Somewhere beyond the Milky Way Galaxy. It was hard to believe that the last twenty-four hours had been real. She looked at Hercules trying to make sense of his sudden appearance. If he was there, then maybe her family was there, too. She searched the pod for them.

"They're not here," Blue said.

"How did you—you read my mind?" Lyra accused. Tears threatened to fall again. She hadn't cried that much in her entire life. All she wanted was to go home and be with her family.

"It was only an assumption. The way you looked at your dog, then around the room."

"How did Hercules get here?"

"I went back to your home to look for clues. He was waiting at the front door. I couldn't just leave him. He can't stay long, but I thought you'd like him near while you heal."

"Thank you. And my family?" Lyra asked.

"We have a rescue team working on a plan. We are doing everything we can. Master requested a meeting with you this afternoon. Archer will meet us there. Do you feel well enough to walk?" Blue asked.

"I'm fine," she quickly replied. "I need to know more about my family. We can't waste time. I would like to see Master now," Lyra demanded, trying to make her voice sound strong and unwavering.

Blue's eyes sparkled with laughter. "Easy there. First, you need to eat and get changed. You can't see Master like that," he motioned to her gown. "I brought you new clothes. Nebula will be here with your food and make you more tonics." Blue placed a fresh set of clothes on the chair next to her bed.

"I'm not hungry. I'd like to see Master and get answers first." She stood up, testing out her legs. To her surprise, she felt completely normal, maybe even stronger. She walked a few steps closer to the chair, thankful for the change of clothes.

"Master only holds meetings on her time," Blue said with caution. "I'm sorry, Lyra, but she will not see you a moment sooner."

"I guess I don't have a choice then. Thank you for the clothes. These look…" she said, holding the clothes at different angles, "they don't look like clothes I'm used to wearing. How do I, um, well, um—do you think Nebula will help me figure out how to put them on?" She carefully laid out the beige tunic-like shirt, and tan pants on the bed. There were strange wraps and straps hanging from them. She left the sand-colored boots on the floor.

"I'm sure Nebula would be glad to help. It's not as complicated as it looks," Blue laughed then pointed towards a smaller wall of metal. "The wash pod is in there. Everything you need is set out. Knock twice on the door if you need anything."

"Will anyone appear out of thin air while I'm in there?" Lyra cringed at the thought of someone appearing in the pod while she was changing.

"No, certain pods have restrictions. No one can bend into a wash pod. You start training after you meet Master. Go get washed up, you need it." Blue scrunched his nose, waving his hand in front of his face. He tried to look serious, but a subtle grin appeared.

"Very funny," she said.

As she approached the wash pod, the wall parted as if by magic. Before stepping inside, she glanced at Blue. With a single nod, he encouraged her to keep going. The door closed soundlessly behind her and the lights automatically turned on. She stood in a small, windowless pod.

The strangeness of this world was overwhelming. She knocked twice, testing to see if Blue was still there.

"Already?" Blue responded from the other side of the wall.

"That was a test. I'm going to shower now," Lyra said, her words came out in a nervous rush. She told herself that she had nothing to be afraid of. She would shower, meet Master and train.

"Yes, please do us all a favor. You stink worse than a newly hatched pterodactyl on a humid day," Blue chuckled.

"Pterodactyl? What?"

"I thought you were in a hurry." Blue's voice grew fainter, indicating he had walked away.

After a quick shower, Lyra wrapped herself in a strange oversized towel and knocked on the door again.

"All done?" Nebula asked.

Lyra was grateful that Nebula answered. Shyly, Lyra said, "Um, kind of. I can't figure out how these clothes work."

"Once you're in the tunic and pants, come out and I will show you how the rest goes. I'm the only one here."

Lyra did as Nebula instructed. She walked out of the wash pod with straps hanging while holding the boots.

"These are basic training suits made from plant fibers. Once we know what your skills are, your clothes will be custom-made to fit your needs," Nebula showed Lyra how the wraps and straps work. "The fabric stretches with your movements. It's very durable. These wraps add a layer of protection while the straps hold your training weapons. The wrap can be used as a compression bandage in case of injury."

"Why are they made from plants?" Lyra asked.

"The plants grow in abundance here. Plant fibers make versatile clothing and can be dyed various colors. We prefer natural and muted colors. These suits offer comfort, strength, and temperature regulation," Nebula replied.

"Oh, that's cool," Lyra said.

The idea of other planets having life and beings on them, much like Earth, had never occurred to her before. She realized how little she knew of the universe. Her mom and dad would find Alora fascinating. Thinking of them brought tears to her eyes. She took a deep breath, promising not to cry again. She was determined to get answers and save her family.

After Lyra finished getting the boots on, Nebula offered to braid her hair. Nebula carefully untangled the knots in Lyra's long curly hair before weaving it into double braids. She thought how her mom would love to see her with her hair free from her face. She fought the tears, quickly wiping them away before Nebula could see. She couldn't control her emotions when she missed her family.

"What is training like?" Lyra attempted to change her train of thought.

"Training can help your skills manifest. You'll learn how to use a part of your mind you've never used before. You'll start with the basics. First, you need to fuel your body and mind." Nebula motioned towards a tray of hot soup and colorful tonics.

In a matter of minutes, Lyra was finished. "Let's go."

Nebula giggled softly. "Your furry family member needs to stay here. Master's orders. I left food and water for him."

Hercules looked up as Lyra patted him on the head. "I'll be back soon." As if understanding, he jumped onto the bed and rested his head on the pillow.

The moment she stepped outside, she was greeted by a gentle breeze. Her training suit allowed air to flow through, cooling her down. She tested the boots on the rocky terrain. They felt both light and sturdy. Nebula was right. The suit and boots were incredibly comfortable.

The first thing Lyra noticed were the tall rocky walls. She had to crane her neck to catch a glimpse of what lay beyond. Alora had a barren landscape with rocky outcrops and little vegetation. The rocky walls seemed to stretch endlessly towards the sky, disappearing into a thick layer of clouds. She looked down the alley, which was as wide as a highway, but strangely empty of any signs of life.

"So, is Master a person?" Lyra's voice echoed as they walked deeper into the alley. There were evenly spaced deep grooves. It made Lyra think of the Oregon Trail and how the wagons left lasting marks on the ground. She learned about them last year in school. She wondered if these were made by wagons.

"A person? Do you mean to ask if she's human? Wouldn't you be considered an alien on Alora?"

"Um. I hadn't thought of that. I guess I would be," she laughed.

They walked the rest of the way in silence. The absence of people made Lyra uncomfortable. She couldn't quite put her finger on it, but she had a strange feeling.

"Nebula?" Lyra said.

"Yes, my beautiful star?"

"Is it always like this?"

"Not usually, no," Nebula responded without looking back.

"Where is everyone?" Lyra asked.

"Waiting for you and Archer."

"Waiting for us? Where is Archie?"

"He's probably on his way from the training arena. We're meeting him at the Grotto."

Lyra felt a pang of jealousy hearing that Archie had been training without her. She wondered if he had been doing well, like he always had in school. She was anxious about training. Would she face the same struggles she did in school? She was afraid of being humiliated. What if she couldn't learn as quickly as Archie?

The path veered off the main road. Archie stood, patiently waiting, his gaze locked onto her. At the end of the path, there was a massive metal wall that marked the entrance to the Grotto. Conflicted, she debated whether to run up to him and make it awkward or play it cool.

"Hey," Archie said.

"Hey," she replied, playing it cool.

Nebula cleared her throat. "Remember not to speak until you are spoken to. Be aware of your surroundings and keep your guard up." She gestured for them to enter.

The metal doors sealed shut behind them, separating them from Nebula. Lyra wondered if Nebula's words were a warning. She scanned the dimly lit hallway as they walked further in. Her palms became sweaty, and she felt the hairs on her arms stand up. She glanced at Archie, only to find his emotions impossible to read. She could always tell how he was feeling. Something was seriously wrong.

Lyra continued to follow him, fidgeting with her bracelet. The lights were spaced further apart making the hallway grow darker.

"Can you feel that?" Lyra whispered.

Archie signaled for her to be quiet. She had a multitude of questions, but she remained silent.

Lyra nearly collided into him when he stopped. "What——," she protested, but he quickly silenced her with a finger to his lips.

The corners of her mouth turned down and she narrowed her gaze at him. As soon as she opened her mouth to speak, Archie pointed at the wall in front of them. The door slid open. He motioned for her to follow. Every fiber of her being begged her to flee, but she wanted answers and this was the way to get them.

Inside the pod, there was an eerie silence. All that could be heard were the gentle echoes of their steps. Archie was barely visible, but she could feel the warmth of his hand reaching out to her. Squeezing his hand brought her a sense of calm.

"Welcome." A friendly voice echoed around them.

"We appreciate your hospitality." Archie's voice lacked emotion. Lyra tried to pull her hand away, but his grip held firm. Panic welled up inside her. This person was an impostor.

"And your friend?"

Lyra forced the words out. "Thank—thank you for the invite." Despite her efforts, she couldn't get free from his grip. Nebula warned her, but did she know who this person was? Where was Archie?

"Please, call me Galena. Master was my father's name. As you know, Helix and Blue are your protectors. They've kept me updated."

"Oh, is your father here? I was told I would meet Master," Lyra said.

"My father is no longer with us. I am the ruler of Alora now. I wish to separate myself from the name. My father ruled harshly, punishing those who spoke against him. Fear gets results, but he ruled without heart and without fairness. My people call me Master out of fear. In time, they will heal and learn that I am not the same ruler he was. Many lost their lives and loved ones during his rule. I wish to restore peace and unity to the Aloran people."

"It would be nice to see who I'm talking with," Lyra said. The person holding her hand yanked hard. "Ouch. Let go of me."

"Release her," Galena commanded.

Without hesitation, the person obeyed. He stepped aside, putting space between them.

"You and I both know that is not Archie," Lyra spoke sharply. She didn't care if she was only supposed to speak when spoken to. She needed to show she wasn't afraid.

She took a few steps backward, putting more distance between her and the impostor. She stopped when she bumped into an icy wall. It felt good against her sweaty palms.

She needed an escape plan. Her body was desperately urging her to leave immediately. Her heart thumped loudly in her ears and she felt a familiar tug of coldness. She instantly knew what she had to do. Her limbs ached as they prepared to bend. She quickly thought of the healing pod, imaging it in her mind.

A strange noise broke her concentration. Something was heading towards her. The room was shrouded in darkness, making it impossible to see. The noise grew louder as it neared. To stop herself from trembling, she lowered herself to the ground. Inhaling deeply, she once again felt the cold air nipping at her skin. Whatever was heading for her was massive, and she had no intention of waiting to find out if she would be its next meal.

Her eyes shut tight as she focused on the healing pod. She might not make it out in one piece, but staying there was not an option. The coldness was so intense that it felt like needles were piercing her skin and pulling her body apart. She embraced the feeling, surrendering to its power.

In an instant, the coldness was replaced by a gentle, tingling feeling. The wind surrounded her, making her body tremble and whirl uncontrollably.

A voice called out her name right before she was ripped away. Darkness consumed her world and she was numb.

~Chapter 6~

"I don't know what you were expecting, Master." Lyra recognized Nebula's voice. "She wasn't ready. She's lucky to be alive. Growing back bones was easier than this. It's unfair that she's has to go through this again. Punish me if you must, but I won't apologize for speaking my mind."

That didn't sound good. Growing her bones back had been a painful experience. One she wished she could forget. If Nebula said this would be worse, she didn't want to know. At least she made it back to the healing pod alive.

Once again, she couldn't open her eyes. Not only did they feel too heavy to open, but something covered them. She couldn't move any part of her body. It was as if her body completely shut down. Lyra didn't like being in this state, yet this time she had no one to blame but herself.

"That wasn't supposed to happen. As soon as she exposed the impostor, the lights would come on. She didn't say anything so, we sent three Archies towards her. I assumed the gluonlets would actually work this time. According to Blue, her skill saved her life again. Why didn't the gluonlets work?" Galena sounded more concerned than Lyra expected she would.

"I don't know why they didn't work. Thankfully, she conserved her oxygen again. But this shouldn't have happened. You shouldn't have tested her like that." Nebula's voice was thick with anger.

"You're aware that Lyra and Archie have a vital part to play in the battle against Saros. Testing them could expose their skills sooner. I need to figure out why Saros wants them. It would give us the advantage. Our time is running short. Her power is increasing day by day, putting my people and this galaxy in grave danger. If she continues to collect skills, she will be an unstoppable force. I needed to try. That's not to say I don't regret it. I wouldn't have tested her if I thought she would end up here again," Galena said.

Lying there unable to move was frustrating. Lyra wanted to scream. She heard footsteps near the counter, imagining Nebula preparing more tonics and solutions for healing. There was a period of silence, with only the sound of Nebula grinding herbs in the stone bowl.

"Master was my father," Galena said, breaking the silence. "Trust is earned, not given. I won't push her or Archie again. It was a careless decision made from fear. Please accept my apology and please call me Galena. I want to earn your respect."

"Fear is powerful. It doesn't go away overnight. Your father's passing brought relief to the Alorans. We fear that you and your brother were taught to repeat his ways," Nebula paused. "The situation we find ourselves in requires immediate attention. Our priority is to stop Saros, but we cannot harm these innocent children. They didn't ask for this. We need to build their trust. Without them, we don't have a chance against Saros."

Lyra realized they didn't know she could hear them. They were speaking too freely in front of her. She hadn't realized how desperate the situation was with Saros until now. When she could move again, she would hug Nebula for her kind words.

"I haven't forgotten their role in this. We will rescue their families and make this right. Thank you for your honesty, Nebula," Galena vowed.

"Thank you for the opportunity to speak freely and without punishment," Nebula said.

"Of course. Let me know when Lyra wakes up. I'll apologize to her in person."

Lyra heard a clicking sound fairly close overhead. It had to be that gadget thing Nebula uses to see internal cell damage.

"It's going to take more than what I have to heal her." Nebula said.

Since Galena already left, Lyra knew Nebula had to be talking to herself.

Nebula went on, "Lyra is left in a state of physical mess while poor Archer thinks he's crazy. She shouldn't have allowed that Walker to use a forbidden manipulation skill. What was she thinking? Using a skill to make someone think they're dreaming while controlling them is illegal. The odd thing is that Archer tried fighting it. I hope he doesn't fight the sedative. Once I'm done here, I will slowly wake him and explain what happened. I really hope he doesn't hate me. Oh, thank goodness. You brilliant girl, you beautiful brilliant star! She protected her vital organs, but this—look at her, Helix," Nebula cried out.

Lyra didn't know when Helix arrived. She was glad he had and hoped he would comfort Nebula. Hearing everything Nebula had said was a lot to process. If Nebula's reaction was that emotional, she didn't want to see what she'd looked like. She had trust that Nebula would piece her back together like nothing happened.

"What are we going to do? We are failing them." Nebula's sobbing was heartbreaking.

"We will plead, grovel, and bribe them with expensive toys," Helix said sarcastically.

"You know, you could be serious instead of making senseless jokes," Blue said.

The inability to see someone bend was jarring. Lyra wondered if bending made a sound and if she could hear someone materialize with training. Since she couldn't see what they were doing, she intently listened, hoping they would say things they wouldn't normally say in front of her.

"Can she hear us?" Helix asked.

"No, she's out. I gave her the same sedative I gave Archer."

"Listen, things were already bad and now they're worse. Think these kids will trust us now? We nearly lost this one—again. The other one is unwillingly sedated. I think we have to tell them the truth. I know, I know—we promised Master we would keep quiet, I mean, Galena. Her name may be different, but her actions today were just like her father's. Anyway, these kids should know why they're here and what they're up against. They should have a choice in this," Helix reasoned.

"Their decision was made for them the moment Saros awakened their minds. It cannot be undone," Blue pointed out.

"Every life in the universe bears the ability to be awakened and manifest skills. Every single person. These kids weren't chosen by the universe. Saros awakened them, so why can't a Walker unawaken them?" Helix said.

She could almost see him walking back and forth, the sound of his footsteps growing fainter as he moved away and then louder as he approached.

"Trying to reverse it would damage their minds. It cannot be undone, Helix," Nebula pleaded.

"Fine, but I will not force them. They will learn the truth and decide for themselves. They can choose to stay and fight Saros or they can return to Earth. I will support whatever they decide," Helix warned.

"They are the youngest Walkers in history. Telling them everything at once could be overwhelming. It's not a good idea," Blue said.

Lyra mentally screamed at Blue for suggesting not to say anything to her and Archie. Maybe he was trying to protect her, but she agreed with Helix. She and Archie had a right to know, especially if they were needed to win this war against Saros.

"You might want to go. When I give her this, the pain could be unbearable and she might wake even on sedatives." Lyra muscles immediately tightened, as if bracing for impact. She focused her energy on moving her hand. If she could make even the smallest movement, maybe one of them would notice. She had to get Nebula's attention.

"I'm not going anywhere," Blue and Helix said at the same time.

It was too late. The solution traveled from her arm, coursing through her entire body.

"Have you done this before?" Blue asked.

"No. This should stabilize her internal pH. If it doesn't, there will be permanent damage to her cellular health. Her bicarbonate ion levels are critically high, which poses a risk of dehydration and potential damage to her heart, kidneys, and brain. She's somehow protecting those organs. For this to work, I need carbonic acid from a meteor. For now, this solution should help a little." Nebula said.

She was hit by a wave of dizziness. Her temperature rose making her overheat, but she didn't feel the pain she thought she would. Maybe the sedatives were helping.

"Should she be sweating like that?" Helix asked. Lyra felt his cool hand on her forehead. "She's burning up."

"I'm starting a slow drip to keep her hydrated. Can you run those rags under cold water? Ring them out and put one on her forehead and one on the back of her neck," Nebula instructed.

"On it," Helix replied.

"I'll get the carbonic acid," Blue said.

"Take this, you'll need it for collection. Be careful," Nebula said.

"I always am," Blue said.

No one talked for a bit. Lyra's head was throbbing, picking up every little sound. Crunching, mixing—Nebula was making another solution.

Lyra heard Helix approach. His footsteps were heavier and he breathed louder than Nebula. He changed the rags, checking her temp before applying new ones.

"She still feels feverish," Helix said.

"She really needs the carbonic acid," Nebula replied. "There are colder rags in the freezer. Try those."

Lyra imagined Helix walking to the freezer. The door squeaked open and she heard the sound of ice crunching beneath his grasp.

"Ready?" Nebula asked. "This second round might be more intense."

Nebula was right. The solution burned hotter as it entered her vein. It felt as though a fiery flame consumed her entire being. She wanted to scream and make it stop. She was convinced that she was actually on fire.

Lyra attempted to block out the pain by focusing her mind. Her mom said the mind could make her believe anything she wanted. She wanted to believe this intense burning would soon stop. It was hard to focus on anything as the pain raged through her body. She forced herself to imagine pulling her mind away from the fire. Then she envisioned enveloping her mind in a protective bubble, unexpectedly numbing the pain.

"What's happening?" Helix demanded.

"She's in pain. There's nothing more I can give her until Blue gets back. Her body rejects the pain medicine, even the ones I've tried from Earth," Nebula said. Lyra faintly heard a sniffle.

"I can help," Helix announced.

A cool wave crashed against her protective bubble, immediately washing away the remaining pain. She hesitantly opened her mind to scan for injuries. Her body felt calm, as if she hadn't just been on fire. She couldn't believe how moments ago the pain went from unbearable to barely noticeable.

"Her heart rate is returning to normal. Keep doing whatever you're doing." Lyra could sense Nebula's disbelief. "How are you doing that? Helix?"

Using every ounce of mental strength, Lyra pried her eyes open. Her vision adjusted as she blinked, allowing Helix's face to slowly come into focus. His brows furrowed and sweat dripped down his face as he held her hand. He was grinding his teeth, doing a terrible job trying to the hide the pain.

"Welcome back, my beautiful star," Nebula said, but her attention remained on Helix. She stood close to him with her hand resting protectively on his shoulder. "Let's get you to a bed."

His hands trembled as he let go and leaned back in the chair. He struggled to breathe as he spoke. "She's the toughest person in this entire universe."

"Helix? How?" Nebula asked, preventing him from falling off the chair. "Bed first, then I will get you pain meds."

Helix gritted his teeth through the pain. "Pain meds. Now!"

Lyra felt helpless. She tried to sit up, but Nebula pushed her back down. With one final exhale, Helix collapsed forward and landed on the ground with a loud thud.

~Chapter 7~

Lyra woke to her stomach rumbling. She sat up, finding a tray with soup and tonics next to her bed. Nebula had been giving her several solutions in her IV of the carbonic acid that Blue brought back days ago. She also had to drink many colorful tonics. She felt stronger every day and was thankful Helix didn't need to take the pain from her anymore. He'd left the healing pod by the time she woke yesterday and hadn't returned since. She wondered if he regretted enduring the pain that belonged to her.

Lyra pulled the tray closer to her bed, inhaling the sweet aroma of the soup. The first spoonful tasted familiar, like something her mom made. She finished it as fast as she could. She was determined to finally train if she could convince Nebula that she was ready.

Archie was not in his usual spot next to the window. For days, he stubbornly refused to leave for training. He didn't bother hiding his anger. It took a bit, but Lyra convinced him to get his negative energy out in the training arena. She knew it was better for him to do something than to stay there fuming. Not being able to go with him still stung.

Hercules kept her company. He ate and slept beside her, only whimpering to go outside for a quick restroom break. Having him there brought her comfort. She missed her family and he reminded her of home.

"Will Helix be back soon?" Lyra asked.

"He went home to visit his family. He has a son around your age," Nebula replied. She was busy disinfecting the healing pod. A family came in a few days with two sick children. They stayed in separate part of the pod to keep exposure down. Nebula took extra precautions to ensure that no one else became infected.

"He never talks about him," Lyra said.

"Not often, no. Oh, I have good news. Your internal pH is almost within the normal range. Your body will finish healing over the next few days. I know you're excited to train, but you need more time to gain your strength. It might be a few more days."

"That means no more solutions?" Lyra couldn't hide her excitement.

"No more solutions. You'll have to keep drinking the tonics for a bit."

"I feel good enough to train today," Lyra said.

Nebula sighed. "Your body has been through a lot. Rest today and I'll consider it for tomorrow."

Lyra breathed out heavily, expressing her frustration. She thought she would be able to leave the healing pod today. Since there was nothing else to keep her busy, she thought she could get some answers. "Do you think Galena will visit soon?"

"I don't know. She's been quiet since the, um, the accident," Nebula replied.

"Have you heard anything about my family?" Lyra asked.

Every time she thought about them, she had to hold back tears. The more time it took to heal, the more time it would take to rescue them.

"We know where Saros is keeping them and Archer's dad, Mr. Seren. I'm afraid that's all I know."

"Does Archie know about his dad?" Lyra asked.

"Yes, Blue told him this morning after it was confirmed that Mr. Seren was captured as well," Nebula said. "Don't move." She replaced the IV with a small bandage and applied pressure.

They both turned when Archie walked into the healing pod. He locked eyes with Lyra. "We're leaving. Are you ready to bend?"

"What?" Lyra and Nebula said at the same time.

With a big sigh, Archie threw his arms up and then let them fall. "You almost died—twice. Galena expects us, a few kids from Earth, to save Alora. This isn't our battle. Blue said we can choose to go home, Lyra. We have a choice."

"You do have a choice, but can I first tell you about Alora?" Nebula asked.

Archie sat by the window. "It doesn't matter what you say. I won't change my mind."

Nebula handed Archie a bowl of hot soup. When he refused, she placed it beside his chair.

"Alectryon, Saros' father, destroyed many planets like Alora many years ago. It's clear that Saros is trying to finish what he started. She will destroy entire planets and anyone who goes against her. She wants total submission so she can become the ultimate ruler. Alora is a refuge to those who lost their homes and loved one in the battle against

Alectryon. We have a duty as Walkers to protect these people. If you go home, Saros wins. You'll never see your families again and she'll eventually go after Earth. This battle is just as much yours as it is ours." Nebula pinched the bridge of her nose in frustration.

Lyra couldn't believe Archie would give up and walk away. "Did something happen today?"

"Why did Saros choose us? Why did she take my dad? Your family? I feel—I feel like they aren't telling us something important. We can't trust anyone. We can figure this out on our own." Archie's head drooped down as he rested it in his hands. This was the first time Lyra had seen him look so defeated.

Nebula looked at Lyra and back to Archie. "Only when new guardians are needed do Walkers awaken another's consciousness. We select individuals from various planets, observing and waiting for the perfect energy match. Typically, we don't wake anyone under the age of 14 Earth years. You two are the youngest Walkers known. It's our duty to maintain balance in the universe. Saros is trying to throw off that balance. You aren't the only ones she's awakened."

"That doesn't answer my question. Why us?" Archie pushed.

Nebula cleared Lyra's tray, pausing at the counter before turning around. "There was a lot of strange energy we picked up on when you guys became friends. Galena sent Blue and Helix to investigate. When they saw Saros, their mission changed to become your protectors. They waited, hoping she would reveal her reasons for frequently visiting you more than Lyra. In the meantime, Saros' soldiers wiped out planet Nora. It was our main training facility for new Walkers. She'd turned some of them to her side, then used them to kill our elite trainers. She's been building an army right under our noses. She's searching for Walkers with rare skills. Even though we don't know what your skills are, we think she's trying to recruit you two to fight for her. That's our best guess."

"This is all for power? Revenge?" Lyra asked.

"Both."

Lyra was at a loss for words. She looked to Archie but he was lost in thought. They had asked for answers and Nebula provided. She continued with her chores while Lyra and Archie processed the new information.

"You're telling the truth. What skill is that?" Archie asked.

"You have a skill called truth intuition. You notice subtle changes when someone lies to you. An increased heart rate, faster breathing, a rise in body temperature, a change in their voice, and even if their mouth went dry or if they're barely sweating," Nebula said.

"We didn't ask to be here. We want to go home," Archie said. "Lyra, can you walk?"

Lyra wasn't ready to leave Alora. She wanted to train and fight for her family. First, she had to show Nebula that she was ready to train. She gave Hercules a gentle nudge and told him to get down from the bed. She swung her legs over the side and slowly stood. She swayed back and forth, before gaining her balance. She'd been in bed way too long, making her legs feel like jelly. Without hesitation, Archie went to her side and steadied her.

"Careful, my beautiful star. You are not fully healed yet. Please sit," Nebula pleaded. "I know you want to go home, but you need time to heal."

"If she can walk, she can go home," Archie encouraged.

Lyra was determined to prove she wasn't fragile. She cautiously took her first step, finding her balance. As her ankle gave way, she fell towards the ground. Archie caught her at the last moment, resulting in an awkward embrace. A sudden rush of heat and energy flooded through her muscles.

"What was that?" Lyra whispered.

"Try again," he insisted. "You got this." There was something suspicious about the way he smiled. The burst of energy had come from him, but she didn't know how he did it.

Nebula let out an exasperated breath. "You are too stubborn for your own good. My beautiful star, please let your body rest today."

She took a moment to steady herself before taking another step. She closed her eyes and focused on channeling the new energy to her legs. She took another step, this one more balanced than the last. Though her movements were clumsy, her legs obeyed. She was slowly walking towards the end of the pod.

For a moment, she lost her concentration and stumbled forward. Archie sent another burst of energy. Her body reacted instantaneously, causing her to regain her balance. Strangely, she'd forgotten about her arms. They dangled at her sides and she imagined she looked like a Tube man, those wacky waving inflatable things.

Nebula gasped, "How? Only trained Walkers know how to use their mental energy."

Lyra looked at Archie, but he shook his head, not wanting her to Nebula the truth. Instead, she said, "I'm just that awesome, I guess."

Archie laughed, but quickly caught himself and crossed his arms. "She is that awesome. Now let's go."

Nebula touched Lyra's arm just as she was about to reach the wall. She knew Nebula would use her skill and find out what they did. "Fascinating. There's an extraordinary amount of energy here. Some yours—" She turned then to Archie, "Archer Seren, aiding her does not mean she's ready. She needs to heal."

Archie's eyes narrowed and his mouth formed a thin, tight line. Lyra knew he was angry. She felt relieved. She didn't know how she was going to tell him she wanted to stay. She couldn't abandon her family. She needed time to think.

Nebula guided Lyra back to the bed, somehow clearing away the extra energy. She nearly collapsed onto the bed, feeling achy and exhausted.

"I will send word to Galena, requesting her presence. You deserve a better explanation. Lyra, rest. Please, don't try that again until I clear you. Agreed?" Nebula was already at the counter gathering tonics on a tray.

"Agreed," Lyra replied. She didn't have to look at Archie to feel his disappointment.

Archie was pacing near the door. He looked like he wanted to run.

Lyra wasn't sure how to make it better. She only knew how to change the subject and focus on something else. Since Nebula gave them a lot of information already, she asked an easier question. "Why do you call me a beautiful star?"

Nebula laughed. "We are all made from the same elements found in stars: nitrogen, carbon, oxygen, hydrogen, phosphorus, and sulfur. These are the building blocks of life and date back billions of years. It's also why we look alike. Every single being in the universe share the same elements found in stardust. The differences between us come from the variations in element percentages."

"So, we're literally stars?" Lyra asked.

"Exactly." Nebula handed Lyra a greenish-blue tonic. "It will soothe your achy muscles. I'm sorry I can't answer all your questions. Not all answers are mine to give. While we wait for Galena, would you like a brief history about skills and bending?"

"Fine. Only to pass the time." Archie sank into his usual chair. He'd never refused a chance to learn.

~Chapter 8~

Lyra propped a pillow behind her, as Hercules rested at her feet. She silently hoped Nebula's story would give her some answers. Would she ever learn to bend without getting hurt? How would they rescue her family? Did her struggles with reading, remembering things, and spelling affect her bending? She was too embarrassed to ask Nebula that last one. Maybe she'd get her answers and then she and Archie could figure out the rest together.

"Ok, to start, you already know what skills are, yes?" Nebula raised an eyebrow. They both nodded.

"Good. Did you know that two people with the same skill might not be equal in strength or ability?"

"No, but it makes sense," Archie said. This time when Nebula handed him a bowl of soup, he accepted it. "Thank you."

"Practicing a skill is like working out. The more you practice, the stronger your mind will be. A practiced mind can use their skills quicker, with better control and effectiveness," Nebula said.

"Skills are like magic?" Lyra asked.

"When something extraordinary happens, it's often referred to as magic. On Earth, some Walkers are known as magicians. They use their skills to entertain and wow their audience. So, yes, skills are like magic."

"You once said that Walkers are awakened to balance the universe. Now that Saros has unbalanced things, are more Walkers being awakened?" Archie asked.

"Yes, however, I think it's best if we go back much further. Alectryon rose to power like Saros, by secretly building an army. His followers were promised power and riches," Nebula said.

"Alectryon is Saros' father, right?" Lyra asked.

"He was. No one suspected what he was doing until it was too late. During a time of peace, he secretively turned thousands of Walkers to join him. Within a short time, they controlled hundreds of galaxies, all of which had Earth-like planets. Millions of beings and creatures were destroyed or forced to call him their leader, including non-Walkers. Alectryon was a force to be reckoned with. It was a very sad time in our history."

"How did you defeat him?" Archie eagerly asked.

"I'll come back to that. Keep in mind that Walkers have a limited amount of energy. To bend between galaxies, we need to rest and restore our energy. As Alectryon either seized complete control or brought utter destruction within a galaxy, some beings and creatures sought refuge on other planets. Regrettably, a few of those planets turned out to be traps. Despite this, Walkers aided numerous beings and creatures in their escape, yet Alectryon's madness resulted in significant casualties."

"Why would he destroy planets with people on them?" Archie leaned forward in his chair to take the tray of tonics Nebula handed him.

"You can benefit from these, Archer." Then Nebula placed a tray of tonics next to Lyra's bed. "It's time for another round." Taking a hot cup of tea for herself, she smiled and resumed the story.

"He wanted to reset the universe, re-write history and make himself the ultimate ruler. There were only two options, either join him or he would destroy a planet. A lot of beings only joined him out of fear. They wanted to save their families and stop their planet from being obliterated. Those who fought him failed. Only a handful of planets offered refuge knowing the risks." Nebula sighed.

Over the next hour, Lyra and Archie stayed quiet as Nebula continued on about Alectryon.

Alectryon's reign spanned centuries, during which he gained faithful followers and gradually extended his authority over galaxies, ultimately claiming dominion over the vast expanse of the universe. A false sense of peace hung under his command. It seemed like he had succeeded as the ultimate ruler. Occasionally, an opposed Walker got caught, refusing to join him. He made it known that anyone against him would be thrown into a black hole, never to be seen again. It was a death sentence. No one could survive a black hole, not even the strongest Walker.

Nebula faced the doors as they slid open. With one look, Lyra knew it had to be Galena. The two heavily armed guards gave it away. What she didn't expect was how young the ruler of Alora appeared to be. She couldn't have been older than fifteen years old, if they were on Earth.

Nebula stood, then bowed her head. "Welcome, M—Galena."

"No need. Please sit, Nebula." Galena smiled. "I am pleased to meet you, Lyra of Earth and Archer of Earth. I hope you are well."

Archie did not move from his chair, his anger practically tangible. Lyra was unsure whether to stand and bow or stay in bed. She looked for guidance from Nebula, who stood silently.

Galena interrupted Lyra just as she was slowly getting to her feet. "Please, stay in bed. I came to apologize for my thoughtless plan. I shouldn't have tested either of you like that. Am I interrupting a history lesson? Please continue." Galena motioned for Nebula to take a seat.

Galena's bodyguards positioned themselves by the doors as she took a seat. Lyra uncomfortably shifted in her bed, unsure how to act in front of a ruler.

"As soon as Lyra learns how to bend, we're leaving," Archie said.

Nebula gasped and hurriedly grabbed water from the sink. Lyra knew Archie was angry, but his disrespect was unnecessary. She glared at him, expressing her disapproval.

"I wish I knew how to make it up to you and Lyra. I made a mistake. I am very sorry," Galena said.

"Thank you," Lyra replied. She looked to Archie for his response.

Ignoring Galena entirely, he gazed out the window. Unexpectedly, he said, "I can feel your honesty. It won't change our minds."

"I understand," Galena said. Then speaking to Nebula, "Please, continue."

Despite his tense body, Archie looked exhausted. The last few days had been strange for them, so she couldn't blame him.

"While life went on under Alectryon's rule, a rebel army of Walkers formed. There were few, but what they lacked in numbers, they made up in skills. They were known as the Universe Walkers, said to bend further and faster than any other Walker. Of course, this part of the story is only a myth. It's said that they plotted to remove Alectryon from his throne of corruption and bring peace to our universe again." Nebula took another sip of water.

"Like Alectryon, they traveled the universe, gaining support. They did something different, though. While Alectryon let his guard down, they trained the Walkers in ways never seen before. He was unprepared for such a large uprising of highly gifted Walkers." Galena added.

"When the time was right," Nebula continued, "the Walkers attacked his strongest soldiers first. It was a brutal battle. Alectryon became vulnerable after his wife and son were accidentally killed, ultimately leading to his capture. His daughter, Saros, fled. No one knew of her whereabouts until recently. She was devoted to her father. There's no doubt she's trying to finish what he started."

"What happened to the rest of Alectryon's soldiers?" Archie asked.

"Most of them surrendered and asked for forgiveness," Nebula answered.

"I can't stay for long. I will do my best to answer your questions," Galena said.

"Where are our families?" Lyra and Archie asked.

"As you know, Saros has them hidden and heavily guarded. We know they are alive and together." Galena stood, stretching her neck.

Lyra was at a loss for words. She had an odd feeling that Galena was hiding something. Curious if Archie also sensed it, she quickly glanced in his direction.

"Why us? What could she do with two untrained kids? You know I can feel when you're withholding something, right?" Archie flexed his fingers and went red in the face.

"I know. My job as ruler requires me to keep secrets. Why you? We don't know for sure. Skills are passed down from parents to children. Maybe Saros linked a Walker to your distant relatives, or maybe she figured out how to change your DNA. Whatever the reason, she's desperate to get to you both," Galena admitted.

"Change our DNA?" Lyra asked.

"We haven't ruled out all possibilities. She has a lab on a nearby planet. We have control of it now. We found some disturbing experiments, including records with your names. It's written in code. We have Walkers working on it." Galena signaled her guards, who positioned themselves beside her.

Lyra's mind couldn't process the news. "Our names?"

"We could be one of her experiments?" Archie asked. He stood up suddenly and began pacing the entire length of the pod. Lyra knew he would be deep in thought.

Lyra didn't want to think about being someone's experiment. Even with her mind awakened, she still felt like herself. The idea of becoming a Walker through a scientific experiment by her enemy made her feel dizzy and sick.

"That is just a theory. We won't know for certain until we crack the code. We had your blood tested. The results show your DNA has not been tampered with, but DNA can be tricky. It's possible that Saros planned to capture you first, then start the experiment. Either way, we don't have enough information. Don't worry yourselves over it," Galena said nonchalantly.

"Easy for you to say," Archie mumbled.

"I have to go. I'll let you know once I have more information about your families. I hope this increases your trust in me. Once this is over, you'll return to Earth. Being a Walker is part of your identity, but you control your own choices. By staying and training, we can show Saros she chose the wrong Walkers to mess with. I have a feeling your skills will be invaluable to the cause."

"We'll think about it," Lyra replied before Archie could.

"Please do. I have much to show you. Alora is a wonderful planet, full of hidden secrets. If you stay, you'll get to see incredible things that Earth beings consider to be myths and fantasy." Then Galena and her guards were gone.

~Chapter 9~

"We will return as soon as you can bend," Archie said. He waited for her to agree.

Lyra wanted to change the subject, but he would see right through her. Telling him the truth would only upset him more.

"You will, Archer, when it's safe," Nebula said.

Steam rose from the hot cups of tea as Nebula poured them. Before taking a sip, Lyra closed her eyes and breathed in the aroma. It had a sweet, fruity smell with a subtle hint of mint. She was thankful it wasn't another round of tonics.

"If we wait until we get our families back, how do we explain where we went this entire time?" Archie asked. He accepted the tea from Nebula, taking a long sip.

"Unfortunately, they will not be able to keep their memories of this event. We have a Walker with the skill of energy manipulation. Unawakened minds are easier to manipulate. It will be like it never happened and that can be replaced by them thinking they went on a long vacation," Nebula said.

"They won't know that we're Walkers?" Lyra asked.

"It would only make their lives harder. They would either feel like they're crazy for imagining things or if they tell anyone, they would be seen as crazy. For their mental health, they don't need to remember what happened and they can never know that you're Walkers."

"I know it's a lot to ask of you, but this must be kept a secret," Blue said.

Lyra almost fell out of bed when Blue appeared. Archie looked unaffected. She wondered if training had helped him see when someone bends. Instead of asking Archie, she had a more pressing question on her mind. "Blue? Did you find out why the gluonlets didn't work, again?"

"They are still being examined." Blue nodded to Nebula. "Is that a fresh pot of tea?" He didn't wait for her reply. He poured a cup and sat in a chair opposite her.

"Why doesn't Archie need them?" Lyra asked, crossing her arms. She didn't hide her jealousy.

"Skills develop at different rates. You used your protection intuition skill, which saved your life two times, without ever being trained. That's impressive. You'll be in the training arena soon enough," Blue stated.

Thinking about all the times she'd struggled in school, she had to ask, "Is there a skill that can help me with—well, with reading and staying focused? It would be nice to not have dyslexia anymore."

"My beautiful star, you are absolutely perfect the way you are. Skills cannot change anything about you. They are an enhancement of what you were born with," Nebula insisted.

"Having dyslexia is not something that needs to be changed. Embrace it like you would a skill and you'll find the advantages far outweigh the disadvantages. With dyslexia comes excellent spatial reasoning, which means you can comprehend three-dimensional objects that others cannot," Blue smiled.

"I doubt that. Words float off the paper and it makes everything confusing," Lyra admitted.

"The universe functions in layers and the floating words are just one layer your mind doesn't know what to do with—yet. It will. Nothing good happens without hard work. Keep reading and one day the words will stop floating," Blue encouraged.

"Walkers have limits, struggles and faults," Nebula said, handing a book to Lyra.

"Where did that come from?" Archie asked.

"I have the skill of conjuration. I can manipulate small objects to bend to me if I know where they are. It's a fun skill, but limited," Nebula shrugged, then winked at Lyra.

"Interesting," Archie admitted. His brows furrowed down in thought.

Lyra sighed, "Oh goodie, a book." Immediately noticing the unusual shape, she traced the raised words. She turned the page, skimming the words. "I can read it just fine."

"Are any words floating off of the page?" Nebula asked.

"No," Lyra admitted, fidgeting with her bracelet. "You knew that would happen. Why? How?"

Archie reached out for the book. She willingly handed it to him. Like her, he studied the pages carefully.

"Your mind is adapting, my beautiful star," Nebula said proudly. She closely watched Archie.

Lyra was at a loss for words. She sat quietly waiting for Archie to say something.

A few moments later, Archie looked at her. "How did you read this? It's not in any language I've ever seen before." His eyes returned to the book, flipping through its thick pages, scrunching his eyebrows.

"Don't make fun of me." Lyra crossed her arms.

"I'm not. Look again. It's not written in English!"

"He's right," Nebula added. "It's written in an ancient language. You can read this because you have dyslexia. It's easier for you to read three dimensional words. Unfortunately, it doesn't help you with flat English words. Honestly, English is one of the hardest Earth languages to learn."

"I can't read it because I'm not dyslexic?" Archie asked.

"With practice and hard work, you could read this, just like Lyra will read fluently one day." Nebula went to the cabinets to get something.

Lyra watched as Nebula gently draped a blanket over Blue. He had fallen asleep, gently snoring.

"When can I train?" Lyra asked. She wondered if her dyslexia would be advantageous in training. Her perspective on the world was changing for the better.

"Your cells look very healthy under the scope. How are you feeling?"

Lyra stood and stretched. "Maybe a little wobbly, but I'm getting better."

"Good. If you continue to improve, you can start tomorrow." Nebula's attention turned to the doors, which slid open, revealing two teenagers.

"Speaking of training." Nebula waved them in. "Lyra, this is Castor and Pollux. They are in charge of your training."

"Nice to meet you, Lyra, daughter of Earth," Castor smiled.

"Nice to finally meet you. Archie can't stop talking about you. Lyra this, Lyra that," Pollux winked at her.

"Lux, don't start with your theatrics. He simply means that we've heard a lot about you. Archer has been worried," Castor clarified.

Lyra glanced at them. They looked like sixteen-year-old identical twins. They both had dark auburn hair, but she noticed the slight differences. Pollux was slightly taller despite their similar body shape. He also had green eyes, while Castor had one green and one blue eye. Then there were their personalities. Pollux was clearly the playful one, while Castor was reserved.

"Pollux thinks he's funny. Don't mind him. Aren't Castor's eyes cool? It's called heterochromia and it's pretty rare," Archie said.

Ignoring the compliment, Castor asked, "How are you feeling?"

"Tired, actually. We've been talking for a while." Yawning, Lyra sat on the edge of the bed.

"One more day." Nebula told the twins. "It's time for lunch, tonic, and rest. Are you taking Archie to the arena?"

The twins nodded. Nebula walked towards the doors, followed by Hercules.

Archie laughed, "That dog never misses a meal."

"No, he doesn't." Lyra got comfortable, leaning back on a propped-up pillow. "So, what's training like?"

"You'll pick it up quickly. You're good at all the athletic stuff. That's half the battle," Archie said, grinning.

"Ready?" Pollux asked.

"Ready," Archie replied.

Lyra thought she saw Pollux wink at her as he disappeared. She wished she could see the particle breakdown, but understood it would take time.

"Nebula should be back soon. Wake Blue if you need anything. See you tomorrow." Castor said, then he and Archie disappeared.

Shortly after they'd left, Nebula returned with Hercules in tow.

The soup was different this time. It was an orange liquid with small, red, pebble-like objects floating on top. It had a pleasant citrus scent. Lyra was surprised when the pieces quickly melted, leaving a lavender flavor. She quickly finished her lunch, then downed the tonics. Shortly after, she fell into a deep, restful sleep.

~Chapter 10~

The following morning, Lyra noticed Nebula standing near a plant on the counter. Its long roots extended over the side and into the ground. Nebula ran her elongated fingers through her stem-like hair, singling out a few thick strands. Using gentle motions, she directed the strands towards the plant. They wound around the stems, connecting with the plant in a way that made them seem alive.

Lyra watched in astonishment as Nebula's stems greedily drank from the plant. A moment later, Nebula softly tugged on the stem, separating the strands. She held them over a large glass pitcher, allowing water to flow freely.

"Wow," Lyra gasped.

"Good morning, sleepyhead. Thirsty?" Nebula laughed.

"Is that how you get water in here?" Lyra asked.

"No. I use this water for the plants and I get hydrated as well," Nebula said. She handed Lyra more tonics. "Drink. You'll need the energy to train."

"That's right. I get to train today," Lyra said excitedly. She looked around the room for Blue.

"He left last night. Before you train, Galena requested a meeting with everyone. Don't worry, it won't be like the last one."

Lyra downed the tonics, ready to be done with them. Nebula handed her a bowl of bluish-green soup. It had a peculiar smell, not unpleasant, but not welcoming either.

"Are soups and tonics the options on Alora?" Lyra asked.

Nebula laughed. "I am what Earth people call a vegan. Soups are easy to make and full of nutrients. This one will boost your energy and reduce cellular harm while training. It's made from an algae called spirulina." Nebula cleared her bowl away and handed her a set of training clothes. "Off to the wash pod. Everyone will be here shortly."

"They're coming here?"

"Galena thought you'd be more comfortable meeting here."

Lyra felt amazing as she walked to the wash pod. She quickly showered and got dressed. She needed help with the wraps, then Nebula braided her long curly hair while they waited for everyone to arrive. The training clothes felt as soft as cotton, just like her clothes from Earth even though they were made from cultivated plant fibers. Lyra felt like a ninja wearing them. To pass the time, she paced the length of the healing pod.

Taking a seat, she observed the pod shrinking as everyone gathered. Pollux and Castor were tucked away in the far corner. Archie once mentioned their ability to communicate through telepathy. It was called neurobonding, mind-to-mind communication, thought to be exclusive to twins because of their shared DNA.

Archie sat in his usual chair, petting Hercules on the noggin. Helix still hadn't returned, and Blue was nowhere to be found.

Everyone remained quiet as the doors opened. Galena and her guards walked in right as Lyra broke the silence with a question directed at no one in particular. "Can animals bend on their own?"

"It depends on the creature," Galena said as she strode through the doors. "It doesn't end well if they get distracted. Most are not meant to bend. On that note, it's time for Hercules to return to Earth. You won't have time for him while you train and it will be dangerous for him to stay if we're attacked. He would be better off with your grandparents. We have a special collar for the bend to keep him safe."

When Lyra looked at Hercules, he stared back at her with his big brown eyes. Although she knew Galena was right, she enjoyed having him there. He was the only thing she had left of her family. Not wanting to admit it, she agreed Hercules would be safer on Earth. "Can we wait until I can bend? I would like to take him."

"Yes, we can do that," Galena said.

Lyra smiled. "What kind of creatures are here?" Images of monstrous and mythological creatures flashed in her mind.

"There are both dangerous and harmless creatures here. Alora, like Earth's moon, is tidally locked and doesn't spin as it rotates around our sun. The Blaze is hot and sunny, while The Froid is dark and cold. Our water sources come from melted ice in the Froid that flows into the center band. No entry allowed because of the fire breathing creatures in both. Among our creatures are rats, cows, and deer. We also have flying creatures and lots of bugs."

"Fire breathing?" Lyra asked.

Galena nodded, "Earth people call them dragons."

"Dragons?" Lyra said, her eyes wide in disbelief.

"Dragons aren't real," Archie laughed.

"They absolutely are and they're really dangerous," Castor said. "When all of those planets were destroyed by Alectryon, the creatures that could bend found refuge on other planets. Dragons come in different types and sizes. Some have fur, similar to Hercules. Some have feathers, others have scales. There's even a type small enough to fit in your pocket. Here, we only have fire and ice types. They're the largest and most unpredictable."

"Master somehow made an agreement with them. If we leave them alone, they'll leave us alone. No one enters the Froid or the Blaze," Pollux added.

"Understood. So, if dragons are real, are other magical creatures real too?" Lyra asked optimistically.

"Absolutely. Children's fairy tales and myths on Earth depict creatures that exist throughout the universe. Unfortunately, like Walkers, there are very few awakened ones. Alectryon's destruction wiped out most of them," Castor said. He reminded her of Archie. They were both incredibly knowledgeable.

"I can't show you the dragons, but you might see a stratalatus while training," Galena said.

"I haven't seen one yet. What is a stratalatus?" Archie asked. "Does it have something to do with clouds?" Archie was always greedy for knowledge.

"Yes, it does. They are a creature of flight and hard to spot since they blend in with the clouds. I'm sure the twins can point one out if they see one flying over, which brings us to this meeting. I sent Helix and Blue on a mission. They will not be joining us, so let's get started," Galena said.

Nebula held a tray full of teacups and what looked to be cookies. She walked around the pod, offering them to everyone. Lyra examined the cookie, turning it over in her hands. Knowing Nebula, they would be healthy and probably sugarless.

Lyra hesitated, but eventually took a small bite. "Oh, these are good."

"Thank you." Nebula smiled, taking a cookie for herself from the tray.

Everyone's attention shifted towards a tall figure standing in the doorway. He acknowledged the guards, who separated to grant him passage. Despite appearing to be around sixteen or seventeen, there was a distinct air of significance surrounding him. Lyra's attention was immediately drawn to the thick white streak of hair amidst his long black hair, which partially covered his eye. She wondered if he bleached it white to hide his mesmerizing eye color.

She had never seen eyes as golden and fluid as this before.

Lyra blinked twice, attempting to break free from his spellbinding appearance. Their eyes were locked for a tense moment before he smiled and looked away. Although short, it left her with an odd feeling, as though it were a warning.

Galena and he were dressed identically in forest green tunics, desert sandy pants, and tall boots laced to their knees. Even though they wore the same clothes, their unique facial features made them distinguishable. Standing silently, he awaited his announcement.

"Let me introduce my brother, Janus. Janus, these are our new guests, Archer and Lyra." Galena gestured towards her and Archie.

Lyra was uncertain about whether she should bow like Nebula and the twins had. She glanced at Archie, only to find him unaffected.

Galena continued, "Janus was adopted from another planet. My mother passed from complications during my birth and my father wanted another heir should anything happen to me. He is also a Walker."

"I know your stay hasn't been pleasant. We will make up for your initial experiences. My dear sister filled me in on everything. My apologies for not visiting sooner," Janus said.

"Lyra and I are going back to Earth soon," Archie said.

"To my understanding, Lyra hasn't been able to bend without ending up, well, in here," Janus waved his hand in the air. "Are you planning on getting your families back without our help?" Janus asked.

"We won't sit here while our families suffer. We'll figure out how to get them back." Archie turned to Galena. "Lyra almost died getting here, then you staged her second near-death experience. We don't owe you anything." Archie's eyes watered.

Moving closer, Lyra bent down to pet Hercules. She subtly let Archie know she was there for him by purposefully brushing her hand past his leg. She wanted to avoid making it too obvious and embarrassing for him. Although she would rather hug him, she knew he wouldn't be comfortable with an audience.

"Lyra's second accident was my fault," Janus said. "Do not blame my sister. One of my skills allows me to sense a Walker's potential energy. I asked her to perform the test. I thought Lyra had an evasion intuition skill. She would have known how to avoid danger and make it to safety without harm. She has a similar skill, which is why I read her energy wrong. Her protection intuition skill allows her to protect her mind, tucking her consciousness in a tight, impenetrable corner of her mind while her physical body heals. It's a remarkably rare skill, but it wasn't the one needed for the test."

Lyra looked at Galena, her brows furrowed in curiosity as she wondered why she hadn't mentioned that before. If Janus recommended the test and Galena trusted her brother, then Archie was pointing fingers at the wrong person.

"And you think telling us this will…
what…change our minds?" Archie snapped.

"Archie—," Lyra's voice drowned out as Janus
spoke again.

"Archer, your truth intuition skill would pick
up on any dishonesty. You know I speak the truth,"
Janus said.

"Archie. My name is Archie."

"Archer is your given name by your mother.
She was a Galaxy Walker too," Janus said.

"What?" Archie said, confused by what he
heard.

Lyra glanced at him, dumfounded by the news.
She was still processing the idea of having a rare
skill, probably why Saros wanted her. And now she
wanted to know why no one had mentioned that
Archie's mom was a Walker. She stared at Archie
and watched as his head shook slightly from side to
side, like he couldn't understand what Janus said.

"Janus," Galena snapped, her eyebrows
furrowed in disapproval.

Lyra noticed the guards' discomfort as they
shifted on their feet. She swept her eyes across the
room, looking for any clue from the others, yet
their faces remained unreadable. Either everyone
was already aware of the news or they were equally
surprised.

Archie crossed his arms. "If my mom was a
Walker, she would have told me. She wouldn't have
kept that from me. I would have known."

"Janus is speaking the truth. She was a Walker,"
Galena said. "She resigned when you were born.

She was sworn to secrecy not to tell anyone, just like you and Lyra cannot tell anyone that you are Walkers. She was a Walker when my father, Master, was alive. As per our archives, Sarah Seren passed away, but her death was marked as unknown."

"How did your mom die?" Janus asked.

"Janus, that's enough," Galena warned. Janus looked at her, his shoulders rising and falling nonchalantly.

"She got sick and passed away within a month of being diagnosed with cancer. She looked fine the entire time." Archie wiped his tears away with his sleeve.

Nebula went to him, her hands gently tugging him out of his chair, then hugged him. Lyra's heart sank as Archie cried. He rarely talked about his mom. She had no idea what had happened until now.

Lyra's eyes narrowed as she observed Pollux whisper to Castor, "She would have known how to treat herself."

Galena noticed. "Pollux? What did you say?"

Pollux shifted before speaking, "Sarah had the skill of medical intuition. It's in her records. She was a physician and would have known how to treat herself."

"Treatments aren't absolute. I'm sure she did everything she could. Archer doesn't need to hear anymore," Galena said. She turned towards the twins. "Do you have news of Lyra's and Archer's families?"

"They are a few galaxies away. They are together, but heavily guarded. We hope to have a successful rescue soon," Castor said.

"That's nothing new or helpful," Archie huffed. He stood near the back counter, taking a sip of water.

"Training will manifest your skills faster and you will learn basic defense. Saros will not stop until she has what she wants, and right now, that's you two. If you stay, you'll be safer and more effective. If you leave, you're only giving Saros what she wants. She'll have you captured in no time and then they will be no hope for your families. Plus, if we're being honest here, we need you both to stay as a part of our plan in capturing Saros," Galena said.

"So, we're going to be used as bait?" Archie asked.

"Something like that," Janus said.

"Not another word," Galena snapped.

"We should tell them the truth," Janus whisper yelled.

Lyra couldn't stand the idea of being used. "I think Archie will agree that we are not your pawns."

"You need to leave, brother." Galena nodded towards her guards.

Janus raised his hands. "No need. But I must say, keeping the truth from them will not help. Master would be disappointed in you," Janus' words hung in the air as he vanished.

"You expect us to stay after that?" Archie waved a hand in the direction Janus had vanished. "I have to agree with him. If you want anything from us, you need to tell us the truth."

"My brother and I have conflicting opinions. I considered his way, testing Lyra against my better judgment. Since then, I give little thought to what he suggests. But he tells some truth. We are considering setting a trap for Saros by using you both. It's only a thought. We need to develop it further and consider the potential risks. Until then, we wish for you to train. We need you as much as you need us. Together, we will stop Saros and bring your families back," Galena urged.

Archie pressed his lips together tightly, creating a thin line. He shook his head, as if debating with himself. He paced near the counter while Lyra anxiously played with her bracelet.

"Archie, is she telling the truth?" Lyra asked.

Archie nodded his head.

Nebula said, "Castor and Pollux can train you starting today if you're feeling up to it."

Archie sighed. "We don't really have a choice, do we? But we decide when we leave."

"Very well," Galena said.

"We train now," Pollux said, winking as he hopped down from where he was sitting. "Ready?"

Lyra joked, "As long as I don't end up back here."

"Oh, you won't. You have me," Pollux winked.

Lyra's cheeks flushed with warmth.

"Let's go," Castor announced.

~Chapter 11~

Since Lyra couldn't bend, they walked through the bustling village streets towards the training arena. She was in awe as she experienced Alora in full swing for the first time. The streets were filled with the sounds of footsteps and chatter as people went about their day. The markets bustled with activity. People pulled carts behind them filled with an array of fruits, veggies, baked goods, and even clothing. She inhaled, taking in the different fragrances.

This area of Alora was gently touched by the sun. A warm breeze brushed against her face, making Lyra feel more alive than she had in a long time. The fresh air had a mood-boosting effect on her until she remembered why they were passing through the market.

She would have to practice bending. As much as she wanted to learn, there was an underlying fear that she would end up hurt again. She pushed her thoughts aside. She continued exploring the market as they walked. The Aloran people had a striking resemblance to Earth people. They seemed like regular people carrying out their daily routines. Although Alora lacked modern technology such as cars, buses, cell phones, and computers. The scene looked straight out of an 1800s Earth photo, except for the clothing. The Alorans wore clothing that resembled training suits, but with a few noticeable distinctions. Since they didn't carry weapons, they had fewer straps.

Lyra enjoyed seeing people hold their babies while toddlers dashed about with boundless energy. She wondered if the school-aged children attended schools like hers on Earth. She hadn't seen anyone over the age of five or six at the market.

She had to jog to catch up to Pollux, Castor, and Archie. No one in the market paid her any attention as she quickly passed their booths. They were too busy going on about their business.

Just past the village, a network of dirt roads stretched out. Pollux and Castor gestured towards the furthest one on the right, leading the way. They walked for about ten minutes; the sound of their footsteps echoed off the huge boulders. In the far distance, Lyra saw an arch made of rocks surrounded by large boulders. She knew it had to be the training arena.

The twins paused at the entrance and stood directly beneath the arch. Archie smiled warmly, gently taking her hand and guiding her past them. The arena was a wide-open area with nothing in it. Once she entered, she was surrounded by a powerful energy. Her arms tingled with goosebumps.

"Do you feel that?" Lyra asked.

Before Archie could answer, Castor said, "These aren't normal boulders. They're stone quartz crystals which hold energy. We'll show you how to tap into them to help stabilize your energies."

"Why is the training arena so far from everything else?" Lyra asked.

"For the safety of the Aloran people, in case your skills get out of control. Most of the people on Alora aren't Walkers. They don't come out this far and they know to stay away," Castor explained.

"But they know about Walkers?" Lyra asked.

"Yes, there are a few planets that know about Walkers. Alora is home to many peoples from other galaxies. People who were rescued before Alectryon destroyed their planets. Nebula is not from here, neither is Helix nor Blue," Castor said.

"Enough lollygagging. The sooner we get started, the sooner we get off this planet," Archie said. He walked further into the arena.

"Not so fast, hotshot. We need to go over the rules," Pollux said.

Archie stopped in his tracks. "What rules? We didn't go over rules when I first came here."

"Patience, Archer. With more than one new Walker training, it can get, well, messy," Pollux said.

"Fine." Archie crossed his arms and leaned against a boulder. "But first, I need to know what's going on between Janus and Galena. I felt something odd coming from Janus."

Pollux walked away, kicking pebbles with a visible slump in his shoulders. Lyra noticed the mental exchange of conversation between the twins. She wished she knew what they were saying.

Castor sighed. "Their father, Master, was a tyrant. Galena is the transformation Alora needs, while Janus is more like their father. Master died not long before you arrived. Galena knows that Janus is trying to get in her head, making her question her decisions. She's much stronger than he gives her credit for."

"I didn't know they lost their father that recently," Archie admitted. "I was a mess after losing my mom for a long time."

"Why didn't they tell us?" Lyra asked.

"Galena was taught not to show emotions. Her business-like attitude comes from her father, but don't think it doesn't affect her," Pollux said. "So, it's time to go over the rules." He nodded to Castor.

"Rule number one, do not bend on your own. Pollux or I will give you the okay when we feel you're ready," Castor said, looking directly at Lyra. The thought of bending made her wince, the memory of the healing pod still fresh in her mind.

"Two." Pollux held up two fingers. "If you are tired, tell us. Using 100% of your brain is exhausting. We don't want anyone to get hurt."

"Three," Castor said.

"Wait. How are we going to use 100% of our brains?" Lyra asked.

Pollux laughed. "This is going to be a long day. Anyone have popcorn?"

Castor rolled his eyes. "Lux, seriously? They're twelve Earth years young. Training doesn't start until fourteen Earth years and even then, they start with the fundamentals."

"That's not our fault," Archie pointed out.

"No, it's not," Castor said.

Lyra was still stuck on the idea of using 100% of her brain. "I thought humans only use 10%?" she questioned.

Pollux couldn't contain himself and burst into laughter. "That's a myth Earth people believe. Everyone uses 100% of their brain, even if they aren't Walkers."

Castor said, "Think of your brain like it's a computer. The 10% you've heard about is the part of the brain you are consciously aware of, like your thoughts. The rest of your brain is busy working in the background. It's performing basic body functions like breathing, controlling your heart rate, regulating your temperature, and more. Walkers use the mind differently to make traveling through space and time at the speed of thought possible."

Lyra said, "Oh, Nebula explained that before. She just didn't mention we use 100% of the brain. Never mind, I get it. Next rule."

"She explained all of it? What's faster than the speed of light?" Pollux asked.

"The speed of thought," Archie answered. "We increase the mind's energy by redirecting our cells to focus on bending to allow us to travel faster than the speed of light, which is incredibly slow compared to the speed of thought."

"What he said," Lyra agreed.

"Go on," Castor encouraged.

"Walkers technically bend the fabric of the cosmos to get from one point to another. In Einstein's theory of relativity, light bends around the sun because of space. It's not a straight line like

Earth people might think. In the same sense, we bend through space with our thoughts to the next galaxy. We practically walk through space at the speed of thought." Archie was proud of his answer.

"How exactly do our bodies get from one place to another? Maybe if I can understand that, I can learn to bend," Lyra wondered.

"Quantum mechanics and entanglement," Castor answered.

Lyra's face twisted in confusion. "Um, what does that mean?"

"Basically, it's a process that separates the particles in your body and then reassembles them in another place. This process makes a replica in the new place while it destroys the original."

"Destroys? Why would you want that to happen?" Lyra asked.

"You can't be in two places at once," Pollux laughed.

"The quantum field is complicated. Bending is a way to travel at unfathomable speeds and distances, but it's not without risks and limitations. We can only travel to the next galaxy before needing to rest and eat," Castor said.

"Like teleportation?" Archie asked.

"Kind of, not quite, but yeah," Pollux said, shaking his head from side to side and then up and down.

"Are you ever serious?" Archie snapped at Pollux.

Pollux shrugged his shoulders and smiled.

Archie rolled his eyes and then said, "What does using 100% of your mind have to do with physics?"

"Another complex process," Castor said. "Um, your mind transports the blueprints to reconstruct the particles. That's why you must remain focused. Your mind is busy making sure your protons, neutrons, and electrons are replicated properly. Any distractions could mean the loss of an arm or leg. Nebula can help rebuild some things, but not important organs like brains and hearts." He looked at Archie and then Lyra, "Bending is complex. We don't have enough time to go over everything. Today, we start with the basics."

Pollux rubbed his palms together as he spoke. "Now for the fun. This is a game of toss the boulders. Stop the boulders with your mind before they crush every bone in your body. Let's play," Pollux whooped.

"You want us to move the boulders with our minds? Like telekinesis?" Archie asked, his voice calmer than expected.

"Exactly. It's about manipulating particles on a quantum level," Castor said.

"Huh?" Lyra had heard her mom and dad mention words like that. She wasn't sure what it would have to do with moving rocks with her mind.

"You're confusing them, Cas. No one understands your science gibberish." Pollux ran his hand through his hair. "Wait, wait, wait. Forget describing it in words. Just watch me." He closed his eyes and rubbed his temples with two fingers from each hand.

"Is he being serious? I honestly can't tell," Archie said right before a massive rock landed only inches from his foot. Startled, he jumped back.

"Pay attention, Archer," Pollux smirked.

Lyra accidentally let out a giggle. She quickly covered her mouth.

"I'm glad you find it funny. I nearly had my foot crushed," Archie snapped.

"Calm down, Archer. It's all about control. I did that on purpose," Pollux admitted. "It was only a rock. Today you'll move those." He pointed to a mound of boulders. Some were the size of a house.

"Can I try?" Lyra asked. She was eager to prove she could do something right.

"There's no such thing as trying. Let's do this," Pollux said.

For the next few grueling hours, Pollux and Castor helped Lyra and Archie learn how to move rocks from one end of the arena and back. The twins showed them different ways to manipulate particles. Once Lyra and Archie mastered moving rocks, they gradually progressed to moving larger and heavier ones. The exercises left them mentally and physically drained.

"We are almost done. Lyra, you are a quick learner. To end the day, you need to move one of those to the other side of the arena," Pollux said.

Even though Lyra felt completely drained, she was too proud to admit it. Instead, she told Archie to go first, which he gladly accepted.

She sat on the ground to rest, noticing how determined Archie looked. His jaw was set as he walked towards a medium-sized boulder. He stood taller, taking in deep breaths before focusing on it.

At first, nothing happened. Archie's expression went from looking determined to painful. Beads of sweat slowly trickled down his face. He swayed back and forth and she knew he was too exhausted to move the boulder.

She stood, planning to stop him when she noticed the boulder quiver. His arms were stretched out before him. Then the ground beneath her feet rumbled as the boulder shook back and forth.

Frustrated, Archie clenched his eyes shut and allowed his arms to fall limply to his sides. He panted as if he had just run a mile. Then he focused on the boulder again.

"Good try, Archer. Maybe next—" Before Pollux could finish his sentence, a boulder came soaring through the air, silencing him.

With a wide smile, Archie fell to the ground.

"Good job, Archer," Castor applauded, helping Archie to his feet. "Easy now. It takes a lot of energy to move a boulder." Castor handed Archer something from his pocket. "Eat this. It will help."

"That…wasn't…what…I…expected," Archie said, panting heavily. His body trembled as if he could pass out any moment.

"That's further than I thought you'd get," Pollux said.

"Lux," Castor warned. He cleared his throat. "Slow your breathing with your mind, not with your body. Take a bite."

Archie popped the small round thing in his mouth and chewed. "What is this?" He swallowed hard.

Lyra noticed his color immediately returned.

"A salt chew. It balances your electrolytes," Castor replied.

"It didn't taste good." Archie took a sip of water from a bottle he had in his backpack.

"I would have chosen a bigger boulder to throw. It might have impressed the lady more," Pollux winked at Lyra.

Archie's face turned red. Lyra wondered if Pollux said those things thinking it would make Archie want to push harder. If so, it was working. Archie rubbed his temples in frustration and tried again. Her eyes widened in amazement as Archie effortlessly tossed a huge boulder towards Pollux.

There was a loud cracking sound and a plume of dust where Pollux had stood. Lyra froze, wide-eyed with disbelief. Then she heard Pollux's laughter coming from behind the boulder. Pollux was untouched, still laughing as the dust settled and he came into view.

"Ignore him. He thinks provoking people leads to better outcomes. Don't let anger take control. It's dangerous and hard to manage," Castor said.

"You have your way and I have mine. And mine worked. Look at what he did. Well done," Pollux said, brushing the dust off of his clothes.

Lyra couldn't believe Archie cracked the boulder in half. Lyra wasn't sure what to say. She was happy that Archie tossed such a large boulder with little effort, but she was worried Pollux would regret messing with him someday.

Lyra gasped as Pollux's particles shimmered in the air before he came into view right next to her. It was the first time she could actually see someone bend. It was impossible for her to know when someone would bend into a pod or near her, but now seeing what it looks like would make it harder for another Walker to sneak up on her. She hadn't noticed Archie storm off towards the entrance.

Pollux whispered to Lyra, "Hurry. Throw that boulder in front of him so he can't leave."

With surprising ease, Lyra hurled the boulder towards the entrance of the arena. Just as the boulder was about to pass over Archie, Nebula materialized right in front of her, shattering her focus. Lyra's eyes widened at the sight of the crimson bloodstains on Nebula's clothes and hands.

"Watch out, Archer!" Castor and Pollux yelled at the same time.

Lyra's attention snapped back to the boulder. It was spinning out of control, creating a whirlwind of dust and debris.

It all happened so fast. One moment Archie walking towards the arch and the next everyone was surrounding the boulder she'd tossed. Archie was nowhere to be seen.

Lyra sprinted towards them. The boulder had been moved off of Archie when she got there. He was lying on the ground, eyes tightly shut in obvious pain.

"Don't move him too fast. We have to get him back to the healing pod," Nebula said to the twins.

Lyra sank to the ground. "No, no, no. Please be okay. Please be okay." Tears ran down her face.

"Lyra, I need you to listen to me. Get to the healing pod now. We're under attack." Nebula's words seemed so far away. She couldn't move. She remained on the ground. "Pollux, take Lyra back. You must bend. Castor and I will take Archer. Hurry!" Nebula took Pollux's place, supporting Archie's head. Lyra watched as millions of particles shimmered before they disappeared.

"We need to go. Focus on a speck of light like your life depends on it. Nebula needs to focus on Archer, and I refuse to bring her another patient." Pollux's words were sharp and urgent.

Lyra closed her eyes, using all of her mental energy to focus on a speck of light.

~Chapter 12~

Lyra heard Pollux's voice softly repeating, "Open your eyes, Lyra."

She stretched her mind out to carefully assess the damage. Opening her eyes in disbelief, she was shocked to find herself unharmed.

"That's because you were bending with me." Pollux looked pleased with himself.

Lyra nodded. She looked around the healing pod for Archie. "Where are they? They left before us."

"Don't worry. Archer is in reliable hands," Pollux said, looking past her.

Lyra turned to see what caught his attention. Two Aloran guards stood in front of a curtain. She recognized the guards. They were Galena's guards, giving away who was behind the curtain.

"It can't be," Pollux said.

The guards broke their statue-like stance when they got closer. A guard tapped his weapon on the floor twice. "You may not enter."

"What happened? Is that… is that…" Pollux couldn't get his words out.

"We cannot say," the guard said.

Just then, the doors opened. Castor carried Archie to an empty bed. "Lux, help. Hurry."

Pollux rushed to help Castor move Archie onto the bed.

"Where's Nebula?" Lyra asked.

"Getting supplies. She'll get here as soon as she can," Castor said.

Archie laid unconscious as his arm hung in the opposite direction of what it should be. Even worse, his left femur bone protruded from the skin.

Lyra clutched her stomach, taking a few steps back. Even though it was an accident, she felt awful for hurting her best friend. She looked away, unsure of what to do.

She heard a gentle voice telling her to sit. Blue turned her away from Archie towards a chair in the far corner. She heard someone pull the curtain shut and knew that if she turned around, she wouldn't be able to see Archie.

Nebula rushed through the doors holding an armful of supplies.

"Is Galena going to be okay?" Lyra asked Blue.

"She was attacked. What happened in the training arena?"

Blue's question left Lyra feeling nauseous. She leaned forward, holding her head in her hands. "I don't—I mean—I—I hurt him," Lyra admitted.

"He knows it was an accident. Don't worry. Nebula will heal him." Blue sat in the chair next to her.

She wished her parents were there. They always knew what to say and how to make her feel better. She needed a distraction. "Who attacked Galena?"

"We're almost certain it was Janus. A guard saw him flee the Grotto. Helix went after him. For now, this is a secret. We need to find out why Janus would do this."

Lyra stayed quiet. She stared at the closed curtains, her eyes following the dancing shadows, fully aware that Nebula was tirelessly working to heal him. She sat there, feeling helpless.

After a few moments of silence, Blue patted Lyra on the leg before walking towards the guards. Pollux was denied entry earlier, but the guards didn't stop Blue. He disappeared behind the curtain.

It felt like an eternity before Nebula emerged from behind the curtains. Lyra shot to her feet, hoping for good news.

"Broken bones heal. He'll be back to training in no time," Nebula said.

Lyra gasped for air, only then realizing she was holding her breath. "Is he in pain?"

"No, he's not, my beautiful star," Nebula said. "The pain-reducing herbs are working. He'll remain asleep through the worst of the healing process. You can go in."

"Thank you," Lyra said, letting the tears fall. "Hopefully, he'll talk to me after what happened."

"He woke during the bend. We had to stop so I could get a sedative. Castor said Archer kept asking if you were okay." Nebula smiled.

Those words opened a flood of tears. Lyra put her face in her palms, trying to calm herself. Nebula walked closer and pulled in for a hug. "He's going to be okay, my beautiful star." Nebula waited until she stopped crying. "Go on. I have to check on Galena."

Archie was covered in blankets up to his chin, hiding his injuries. Seeing him look so peaceful and hearing his soft snoring made Lyra feel better. She took a step closer, watching him for a moment before she settled into a chair near the bed. She planned on staying until he woke. She wanted to hear from him that he was okay and wasn't mad at her.

For the rest of the day, Nebula busied herself with taking care of Galena, Archie, and a few other patients. She made tonics, solutions, and brought her gadget to observe everyone from bed to bed. Lyra stayed out of the way and asked for nothing. Hercules stayed near her, only nudging her when he needed to go out or wanted something to eat.

Just when Lyra's stomach growled, Nebula placed a tray next to her. It had a bowl of steamy blue soup and a few tonics. Nebula took a tonic for herself.

"Thank you." Lyra pulled the tray closer. "How's Galena?"

"She was badly hurt. Her wounds are deep and I'm afraid even after she heals physically that she'll need more time to heal mentally."

"What happened?"

Nebula sat on the edge of Archie's bed, not disturbing him. "Helix and Blue returned to give her an update, but they found her, well, it wasn't good. All signs point to Janus. Galena's pod is warded. No one can bend in or out of it without knowing how to get past the wards. We've warded the healing pod now too." Nebula sipped from her glass.

"What was the update?" Lyra asked.

"It's not good news, I'm afraid. They were close to rescuing your families. They came back for Galena's approval and to grab supplies, but everything changed after finding her like that. They put a call out to other Walkers, but by the time help arrived, it was too late. Saros has been moving your families to a new location every few days. It will take time to find them again. I'm so sorry, my beautiful star."

Lyra sat back, taking in the information. If Janus hadn't betrayed his sister, she could've had her family back. She pushed her tray away, standing to pace. She was too angry to sit there. She couldn't believe he'd ruined her chance of her seeing her family. Why did he attack Galena? Nothing made sense. She walked the length of the healing pod and back again. She flexed her fingers before cracking her knuckles. Her face burned as she stomped around. She felt an unstoppable urge to break something, fueled by restless energy. She had never experienced such intense rage before. Using her mind, she lifted an empty bed in the far corner.

"Easy, my beautiful star. That will change nothing. You have every right to be upset. I'm upset for you, but breaking things will not make you feel better." Nebula placed her hand on Lyra's shoulder. "There are clean clothes in the wash pod. Go shower, then rest. Archie won't wake until tomorrow."

Lyra lowered the bed to the floor. A shower sounded like a good idea. She took her time, letting the hot water wash away her tears. She cried until she couldn't cry anymore. Then she got dressed and returned to the chair next to Archie's bed. She wanted to do more. She wanted to be useful.

When Nebula came to check on Archie, Lyra asked, "Can I see Galena?"

"Come." Nebula smiled. "Lyra has my permission to enter." The guards nodded, opening the curtains.

As soon as she walked in, Lyra went to fidget with her bracelet, but it wasn't there. She looked around, squinting at the floor in case it fell off.

Blue, who was sitting near Galena's bed, asked, "What are you looking for?"

"My bracelet. I never take it off."

"I'm sure it will turn up." Blue said.

Lyra assumed it would be somewhere in the healing pod and would look for it when she went back. She sat down to ask Blue about Galena, but he looked like he hadn't slept in days.

Lyra looked at Galena as if seeing her for the first time. Her golden-brown skin glistened with tiny droplets of sweat. Blue stood to move Galena's violet-colored hair to the side of her face. He put a cool towel on her forehead, then sat back down.

Even though Galena could pass for a teenager on Earth, there were a few minor differences. Her eyes were slightly further apart and larger. Her movements could be odd at times. It was like she had more bones and could move them in unique ways. Then there was the star-shaped scar on her neck. It was raised and darker than the rest of her skin.

"It's a symbol of royalty," Blue said.

"Do all the rulers have them?"

"No, it was Master's idea. He branded Galena and Janus with the star when they were young. He wanted other Walkers to know they were royalty. It makes sense why Janus attacked her. He wants to rule as his father did. He thinks Galena is too soft and undoing what their father had done. Master raised them both as leaders. Two leaders with opposing ideas are a recipe for disaster, especially when Janus thinks he deserves to rule."

"Why would he deserve it?" Lyra asked.

"He was adopted, but he is older than Galena and the title goes to the eldest. However, Master never re-wrote his wishes, so the title fell to Galena. They both feel the title is rightfully theirs."

"Oh." Lyra understood why they would debate who should rule, but found harming the family for a title to be barbaric.

They sat in silence. Lyra's hand instinctively reached for her bracelet. Going on the day's events in her mind, she said, "I think I lost my bracelet in the training arena. I need to go back to look for it."

Blue's eyes grew wide. "You *always* wear it, right?"

"Always. Ever since my parents gave it to me," Lyra said.

"You wore it during the bends that went wrong?" Blue asked.

Understanding dawned on her, "Except for this last time when I didn't get hurt."

"Do you know if you lost it before you threw the boulder?"

"I don't remember, but I think it was gone before bending here with Pollux."

"I have to go." Blue walked towards Nebula and leaned in whisper something in her ear. Her face went from shock to concern in an instant. She nodded. Then he walked out of the doors and vanished before the doors shut.

Lyra knew he was going to the training arena to look for the bracelet. She wished he'd taken her with him. She wondered if it really could have been the reason her bends went wrong. She wondered what could possibly be in the bracelet that could mess up a bend. It had to be some mysterious substance or an element that could interfere with her mental energy. Maybe it was something that could stop her from being able to hold her particles together. Sitting there would not give her answers, so she gave Galena's hand a gentle squeeze before going to find Nebula.

"Can I bend to Earth for a quick visit?" Lyra asked.

"Sorry, my beautiful star. I need to be here to care for Galena and Archer. It's a crucial time in their healing and I have other patients to tend to, as well."

"Do you know if Pollux or Castor are busy?"

"I'm not sure if it's a good idea for you to bend until we know for sure that your bracelet was the issue."

"I know, but I didn't get hurt bending with Pollux. Can you ask him to come here?"

Nebula touched her wrist. "I don't agree with you bending. You may talk with him. He'll be here soon."

Lyra scrunched her eyebrows. "How?"

"Alora doesn't have advanced technology, but Walkers need to communicate. These wristbands are called lifelines." Nebula pulled her sleeve back to reveal different colored bands around her wrist. "My fingerprint activates it, sending a signal and my location to the person I choose. This one is a direct line to Pollux. He's training you, so he should know about the bracelet."

Less than a minute later, Pollux rushed through the doors, searching for the threat.

"Everything is fine. Lyra has a favor to ask of you." Nebula never looked up from what she was doing as she spoke to him. She was making more tonics and solutions at the counter.

Pollux quickly straightened and relaxed. "What can I do for you?"

"I need to bend to Earth to get something for Archie," Pollux narrowed his eyes as Lyra continued, "To cheer him up, and I want to get something for Galena too."

"Lyra, we got lucky. Helix will have my head if you get hurt again." Pollux crossed his arms.

"I lost my bracelet before the last bend and nothing bad happened. What if the bracelet was the problem?" Lyra asked.

Pollux tilted his head and paused. "Hmmm, I don't know. It's possible. Where's Blue?"

"He left after I mentioned that to him."

Nebula rushed past them in a blur. She threw the curtains open, and that's when Lyra heard him. Archie was groaning.

"He's not supposed to wake until tomorrow." Nebula held her hands out, and a tray immediately appeared.

Nebula left the curtain open. Archie's eyes were shut tight in pain and he was reaching for his broken arm. Nebula waved Pollux over to help hold him still while she tried to inject something into his IV.

"Easy, Archer," Nebula insisted. "I'm giving you something for the pain. It's okay."

"No. Don't. Want. Anything." Archie dragged out each word he spoke.

Nebula froze. "It will help. Please, try to stay still."

Archie was looking in Lyra's direction, scanning the pod. She knew he would be angry, but she didn't think he would pretend not to see her.

"Archer, it will help you sleep," Nebula urged. Pollux struggled to hold on to Archie.

"I, I'm fine. I don't want that stuff. I can feel it in every part of my body," Archie said.

Pollux stepped back, letting go of him. "Add the anatomical intuition skill to the list. Lyra has it too. That's very interesting."

"Where is she?" Archie scanned the pod again.

"You're looking right at me."

"Where?" Archie asked.

"Um, Lyra? I can't see you either." Pollux scanned the pod.

"I'm standing right in front of you guys. Stop playing around," Lyra demanded, waving her arms in front of her face.

Nebula slowly walked around the pod with her arms outstretched.

"That's not funny. Did Archie ask you to do this? To get me back for what I did? I'm sorry. I'm so sorry, Archie," Lyra cried out.

Nebula lowered her arms. "No one is trying to be funny, my beautiful star. We seriously can't see you. Pollux, is this even possible?" Nebula asked, sounding both concerned and intrigued.

"It's extremely rare. She's bending light around her to make it look like she's not here." He paced, tapping his chin with his pointer finger. "Photo— photokinesis? That's it. Photokinesis. She can manipulate light particles without manipulating her own particles, like when we bend."

Archie pushed himself into a sitting position. "How do we get her to reappear?"

"Stop talking as if I'm not here. I'm right here." Lyra clutched her chest. "Can't breathe," she said.

"Can you sit in this chair and reach for my arm? I need you to slow your breathing." Nebula awkwardly held her arm out waiting for Lyra to take hold.

Lyra found it funny to see Nebula searching for her. A snort escaped her. She swiftly covered her mouth with her hands. She didn't stop laughing.

Nebula gasped, "Lyra!"

Rarely did Nebula use her real name. Her heart raced and she felt dizzy again.

Pollux walked towards her. "We saw you for a second when you laughed. Can you do that again?"

"Just as I thought. Your invisibility is triggered by stress, my beautiful star. Take a deep breath and focus on being seen."

"Easy for you to say. I wanted to go home and get something for Archie *before* he woke up. That didn't happen. I wanted to make things better. All I do is make them worse." Lyra didn't care if everyone knew she was crying. At least they couldn't see her. Being invisible had some benefits, she thought. "I'm so sorry, Archie. I never meant to hurt you. I got distracted and lost focus. I want to go home."

"I'm not mad at you. I'm fine." Archie winced as he tried to stand. "I will be fine. I want to go home, too. Hercules wants to go home, too. Don't ya, boy?" He gently patted Hercules with his good arm.

"I'll go find Blue. I can help him with the bracelet and let him know about Lyra's fancy new skill," Pollux said.

"Tell him to forget about the bracelet and come back quickly," Nebula urged.

Lyra wiped her tears away and took slower breaths, willing her heart rate to slow down. The sensation was overwhelming, like tiny pinpricks against her skin. She took in a slow deep breath and let it slowly out, feeling a cool wash over her body. It felt exactly like bending.

Nebula hugged her. "There you are, my beautiful star. Everything will work out."

"No, it won't." Lyra pulled away. She went to Hercules and placed a hand on his head. "My parents, sister, and Archie's dad are still hostages by a crazy ex-Walker who wants to destroy the universe. Everyone here thinks Archie and I can help stop her, but we're untrained and I only make things worse. And now Archie is hurt." Lyra let the tears run down her face. "Galena's own brother attacked her. Helix is risking his life looking for Janus. I just want to go home. Please, just let us go home. Archie doesn't want to be here either."

"You and Hercules should go home," Archie said. His eyes were tightly shut.

"Beautiful star, slow your heart rate. You and Hercules are flickering. Archer, please let me give you something for the pain?" Nebula looked back and forth between Lyra and Archie.

Then Lyra felt a cool tingle and a tug at her particles. At first, she thought she was making herself go invisible again until she noticed Archie was uncontrollably shaking.

"No!" Nebula reached out to her, but it was too late.

~Chapter 13~

"I'm in my house. This is my room!" Lyra looked around in disbelief. "Archie? Archie? Come on Hercules, let's find him."

She ran down the hall, searching the rooms, only to find them empty. On her way downstairs, Hercules pushed past her, barking. Someone was there.

When she turned the corner, she saw Pollux. "You're okay?" He gently grabbed her, inspecting every inch. Lyra had never seen him so serious and concerned. Convinced she was safe, he released her and stepped away.

"I'm fine. Where's Archie?" Lyra asked.

"Still on Alora."

"How did I get here? I know I didn't bend."

"Archie has a new skill. He can apport," Pollux said.

"Apport?"

"He can relocate people or objects to wherever his mind chooses. Hercules went with you because you were holding on to him. Sending you and Hercules is a crazy awesome skill for not being trained." Pollux made his way to the kitchen.

"Wait. The police must be looking for us. My parents haven't gone to work. My sister and I haven't been to school. My grandparents probably think we're dead by now." Lyra automatically went to fidget with her bracelet, quickly remembering she'd lost it. The lights flickered. "No, no, no. Not again. This happened the night we were attacked. Saros knows we're here."

Pollux pulled Lyra behind him, sandwiching her between him and the wall. "There's no threat here."

"How do you know?"

"I have the skill of fight intuition. I can sense negative energy and would know how to fight our way to safety. As useful as that sounds, I can't tell what my opponent will do, so it's not a guarantee."

The lights flickered again.

"Lyra? You're invisible again. Listen, you need to slow your heart rate. I think you're causing the lights to flicker. My job is a lot harder if I have to protect someone I can't see."

Lyra needed to trust him. If anyone had been there, they surely would have attacked by now. She pushed her fear aside and took long, deep breaths.

Pollux smiled. "The lights stopped flickering. Interesting. Time is much slower on Earth than on Alora. Grab what you want then we have to bring Hercules to your grandparents' house. He can't come back with us. I'll be in the kitchen looking for something to eat."

"Good to know. I'll be right back." Lyra ran upstairs to her room. She grabbed her galaxy backpack and threw the things she wanted inside. When she made it to the kitchen, she saw Pollux throwing cheese puffs to Hercules.

"What? He looked hungry. I doubt your grandparents suspect anything. Only a few hours have passed on Earth since you've been gone." He threw another cheese puff to Hercules then ate a few.

Lyra laughed, taking a few cheese puffs for herself. It was good to be home, even if she knew it wouldn't last.

Pollux held out his hand, palm up, cheese puffs in the other. "Hold on to Hercules' fur, not just his collar." Then he gave Hercules a handful of cheese puffs. "This should keep his mind focused. Ready?"

Lyra took his hand. "Speck of blue light." She grabbed a fist full of Hercules' fur.

"Think of your grandparents' house. Think of exactly where you want to go."

She closed her eyes, imaging the walkway leading to their house. A familiar coldness surrounded her. For the first time, she left herself connect to the energy in a way she'd never done before. It was calming and chaotic all at once, and then they were gone.

"You did it." Pollux sounded proud.

"I did?"

"That was all you. I was ready to take over, if need be, but you did this. I really think it was that bracelet."

They stood in front of her grandparents' house exactly where she imagined. The lights were on inside the house. She let go of Pollux's hand, trying to keep a hold on Hercules, but he got away from her. He ran right to the front door, wagging his tail. Lyra's grandma always spoiled him with treats.

"I need to sit," Lyra said when she caught up with Hercules. He nudged her with his nose. She needed a moment to think. What would she say to them? How would she explain everything that had happened?

"You're invisible again. If your grandparents see me with Hercules, they'll probably call the cops," Pollux said.

The porch lights turned on and the door handle slowly turned.

"I—I—I can't. What am I going to tell them?"

"Think of Archie. No, better yet, think of me. Admit it. You like me, right? Like, like me?" he teased.

"Can you be serious for once?" Lyra giggled.

"That's it. Almost there," Pollux whispered.

The door opened just as Lyra fully materialized and Hercules pushed his way in.

"Hercules?" Grandma screamed. "Lyra!" She pushed past the dog and hugged Lyra. "What's going on? Where are your parents? Nova?"

"Who are you?" Grandpa's voice was icy.

"Easy, Gramps. Can we come in to explain?" Pollux smiled with his hands up to show that he meant no harm.

"This is Pollux. We have a lot to tell you guys," Lyra said.

Lyra's grandpa motioned for them to follow. Grandma would not let go of Lyra as they made their way to the kitchen.

The house smelled of peppermint and lemons, just as Lyra remembered. Grandpa settled himself at the far end of the old, sturdy wooden table. Pollux took a seat across from him while Grandma and Lyra sat next to each other.

"Spill it. Who is this?" Grandpa demanded.

"Let's start from the beginning," Pollux said.

For the next hour, Pollux and Lyra took turns explaining everything. She wasn't sure if her grandparents believed them or thought they were crazy. Either way, they listened without interrupting.

Once they finished, Grandpa and Grandma bombarded them with questions. They spent another hour answering every question. Being skeptical, Grandpa asked for proof.

"Do you think you can show them?" Pollux asked Lyra.

"Show us what?" Grandpa asked.

"This is too much. You must be hungry." Grandma excused herself. She got busy making ham and cheese sandwiches.

There was a pitcher of lemonade on the counter. Lyra got a glass for everyone.

"Show us what?" Grandpa repeated.

"Let them see you or not." Pollux winked.

"I don't know if I can." Lyra finished passing out the glasses at the same time Grandma handed everyone a plate with a sandwich and grapes. Lyra's stomach growled. She picked up the sandwich and took a bite.

"You can do anything you put your mind to. They need to see this," Pollux said.

"Is it dangerous?" Grandma asked.

"Not at all. It's just, well, it's not something I've done on purpose."

"What are you talking about?" Grandpa asked.

Lyra sighed. "Okay, I'll try. Please don't eat. I don't want anyone to choke when you see this."

Lyra closed her eyes, searching for the right energy and pull. When she felt it, she slowly opened her eyes. Pollux's piercing blue eyes met her gaze, offering encouragement. With confidence, she winked before disappearing.

Grandma's mouth dropped open in shock, hands instinctively covering it. Grandpa's eyes widened, his mouth gaping open in disbelief. He tightly gripped the table's edges with his hands. They remained silent.

Lyra reappeared, unable to suppress her laughter. "I'm okay. See? Well, now you don't."

"Stop. We believe you." Grandpa's face turned pale.

Lyra reappeared next to him, startling him. "Sorry. I won't do it again."

Pollux laughed. "You have excellent control. I knew you could do it."

Lyra smiled. "Thanks. I was able to keep my heart rate normal."

"Good. I hate to spoil the fun, but we need to get back. Take care of old Herc, will ya?"

"Of course," Grandma said. She stood, twisting her hands in her apron.

Lyra smiled, realizing where she got her nervous habits from.

Pollux and Lyra had explained earlier that they couldn't stay long. Grandma's hug stretched on for minutes while Grandpa stayed nearby, sniffling. Lyra didn't want to leave them, but promised to be back soon with her parents and sister.

Pollux finished the last sip of his lemonade before standing. "We're doing everything we can to get the Stewarts and Mr. Seren back."

"Please keep Lyra safe," Grandpa said.

Pollux nodded.

"Please be safe. We love you," Grandma said, wiping her tears away.

"Love you both very much," Lyra said.

"Bring our family back, please," Grandma pleaded, her voice trembling. She stepped closer to Grandpa and he put her arm around her.

Lyra quickly patted Hercules goodbye, then grabbed her backpack.

"This bend is a lot longer. Keep your mind focused and let me lead," Pollux said, stretching his arms out.

Lyra nodded and held tight to his forearms. She focused on seeing Archie, instantly feeling the pull as they left Earth.

~Chapter 14~

Pollux entered the code, opening the doors to the healing pod. Lyra didn't take more than a foot in when Nebula charged towards her with her gadget. Nebula circled her, thoroughly inspecting every inch. Lyra stood still, letting Nebula do her thing. It felt nice to be fussed over.

"She's fine and she has another new skill." Pollux grinned widely. "Is Blue back with the bracelet?" Pollux asked.

Nebula didn't answer until she was done. She moved the gadget away from her face. "You're in perfect health. Remarkable."

Pollux stopped pacing. "I need to find Blue before he bends with the bracelet. Is he in the arena?"

"You guys were gone for a few days. Blue stopped looking for it, but I think he and Castor are sparring in the arena hoping to find it on accident," Nebula said.

"I have to go." Pollux rushed through the doors, disappearing once he was on the other side.

"I'll get you some tonics. Bending uses a lot of energy," Nebula said. She didn't wait for a reply before leaving.

Lyra made her way over to Archie's bed to check on him. His curtain was open.

"Hey. Can I come in?" Lyra asked.

"Sure. No Hercules?"

"We left him with Grandma and Grandpa."

"You got to see them. That's awesome."

"Yeah, but Pollux said they will have to have their minds swept when this is over. It's for their protection or something. Anyway, I'm really sorry for hurting you. I didn't mean to hit you with the boulder." Lyra shoved her hands in her pockets, looking for something to fidget with.

"I know you didn't mean to. Sorry for sending you away like that, but it was pretty cool, huh?" Archie smiled.

"It was more than cool. I should thank you. So, thank you."

Lyra told him everything while Nebula prepared tonics and soup. She was happy that Nebula overheard their conversation, saving her from having to repeat it.

"Wow. Time is so weird. You were gone for a few days here, but only hours on Earth," Archie said.

"It should be called time travel instead of space travel," Lyra laughed. "Oh, I brought you something." She rummaged through her backpack.

With a rosy pink glow on his cheeks, Archie accepted the light blue baby blanket. It was well-loved throughout the years. It was missing its silky border, but it felt as soft as a cloud.

"I can't believe you still have this," he laughed. "I gave it to you when you were really upset, remember?"

"I remember you gave it to me when I needed it most. I know you miss your mom a lot and now your dad. I brought Stuffy for me." With a smile,

Lyra took a scruffy stuffed brown bear out of her backpack. "Oh! I have something for Galena too. Is she awake?"

"Not yet. You can visit her though." Nebula nodded to the guards to draw the curtains back. "It's best to let her sleep through the worst of the healing process."

Archie tried to get out of bed. "I'd like to see her too."

"Stop. You are not ready to put weight on that leg. I'll roll you closer." Nebula unlocked the wheels and pushed Archie's bed.

"I know what happened, but she looks worse than I thought she would," Archie admitted.

Nebula sighed. "Janus threw her into a glass statue. It shattered. Galena landed on the shards of glass and was knocked unconscious when her head hit the floor. She has some deep cuts and lost a lot of blood. Her lifeline band was missing. We think he left her to die. She will physically heal, but a betrayal like this takes time to mentally heal." Nebula gently dabbed a damp cloth across Galena's forehead.

"Why can't Helix take her pain like he did for me?" Lyra asked.

"I'm afraid it's not that simple. She's been having nightmares. I've tried different herbs, but nothing helps. If I wake her, she'll be in a lot more pain. Unfortunately, there's nothing Helix or I can do for her."

Lyra looked at the purple and green stuffed dragon she brought for Galena. She gave it a kiss before gently slipping it under Galena's arm.

"I would rather be awake surrounded by friends dealing with physical pain than alone to face my nightmares," Archie said.

"Me too," Lyra said.

"You too?" Nebula asked.

"I was agreeing with Archie," Lyra said.

"I didn't hear him say anything. You look tired, my beautiful star. Can you push Archer's bed back to his spot? I'll bring over food and tonics when I'm done here."

As they passed the guards, Lyra wondered where they'd been when Galena was attacked. She couldn't say anything to Archie without them being able to hear her, so she continued on. Once his bed was in place and locked, she sat in a chair resting her feet on the edge of his bed. They said nothing while they waited. Soon enough, Nebula brought them a bright blue soup and colorful tonics.

"Archer, what did you say earlier? I didn't hear you," Nebula asked.

"I didn't say anything. I was thinking to myself."

"No, you said it loud enough for everyone to hear." Lyra looked at Archie, scrunching her eyebrows in question. Was he playing games with her?

"I was thinking it and I've been trying to do it again," Archie admitted.

Lyra shook her head, letting him know she heard nothing.

"Open your minds to each other. Try again, Archer," Nebula said.

With closed eyes, Archie became completely still.

Lyra burst into laughter, clutching her stomach. "Stop. I can't. Ouch."

Archie laughed. "I thought you'd like that."

When she was done laughing, Lyra said, "It sounds like you're talking normal, though."

"Amazing. You guys amaze me more and more every day. Walkers have a few skills, but you guys are developing skills faster than any Walker I've known. Oh, I have an idea. Eat. You'll need your energy."

"What's your idea?" Archie asked.

"You need your energy for healing, but I think Lyra should try to communicate with Galena."

"I didn't do anything. That was Archie," Lyra pointed out, bouncing her leg. A nervous habit of hers.

"I think you should try," Archie suggested.

"I'd like you to ask her if she wants to stay asleep or to be woken," Nebula said.

Suddenly, feeling sweaty and claustrophobic, Lyra grabbed a cup from the counter and filled it with cold water. Without pausing, she finished the whole thing. She didn't want to let Nebula down.

Archie suggested, "Let's practice first." He sat up, rearranging the pillows behind him.

"I don't think I did anything, but we can try." Lyra stood in front of his bed.

"Concentrate on what you want to say to me and only to me. Repeat it in your mind," Archie said.

Feeling silly, Lyra stared at him and focused on repeating a short phrase. There was a noticeable mental barrier between them. She visualized a door materializing in her thoughts. Testing it out, she found it unlocked. With a slight push, it swung open. A rush of air pushed her back physically. She immediately slammed the door shut.

"You blocked me," Archie accused.

"You pushed me," Lyra said.

Archie laughed. "I forgot to warn you about that. I manifested another skill while you were gone. It's nothing super useful, but it's cool. I can move air, like make wind happen. Anyway, let's try that again. I'll say something to you."

"Another skill? That's cool. You'll have to tell me how you figured that out after we get this one down. Ready?" Lyra sat down, knowing what to expect. She opened her mind, imagining the same door unlocked between them.

"Is that better?"

"Much. Can you hear me?" Lyra asked.

Archie nodded. *"I think this is what the twins do."* He smiled.

As she opened her mind to him completely, his voice echoed in her head like a surround sound. She heard him on new level.

"I wonder if we can do this from far distances." Lyra couldn't contain her excitement.

"I assume you guys figured it out?" Nebula asked.

"This is what the twins do?" Archie asked.

"They communicate through each other's senses, not in words. It's called neurobonding. Since they're twins and share DNA, they also share similar particles. I think you guys have a different skill—telepathy, which is extremely rare. It requires manipulating particles to carry a message into the mind of another and getting it past their mental walls. It's as if your thoughts bend to the other person's mind to deliver a message," Nebula said.

"We are definitely using this when I need help on a test," Lyra said.

"I am not helping you cheat," Archie said, shaking his head low to hide his grin.

Lyra walked to the far end of the healing pod. *"Can you see what I see?"*

"No, but I can still hear you like you're next to me," Archie laughed.

"I have an idea. Should we try to talk to Nebula like this?"

"That's an excellent idea."

"You go first."

"I can try, but I'm getting tired," Archie said.

"It seems like you guys have the hang of it. Ready to see if you can talk with Galena, my beautiful star?" Nebula handed Archie more tonics.

Lyra didn't answer. She watched as Archie stared at Nebula. *"I can't get through. It's so different. There's a thick fog with pointy spikes that jab towards me when I try to get closer. It hurts."* He held his head, rocking back and forth.

Nebula grabbed her gadget then rushed towards him. "You're sweating. You're depleting too much energy. Walkers have limits, you know? I'll get something for the pain and some cool rags. Use no more energy or you'll risk burnout, and that's not something that can be easily fixed."

"I'll get the rags," Lyra offered.

She put one on the back of his neck, feeling the heat radiate. "I think he has a fever." Then she draped one across his forehead.

"When a Walker is close to burnout, their internal temperature rises, like a fever," Nebula said. She crushed a few more herbs, making a paste before bringing it to Archie.

"I couldn't get past your shields," Archie whispered.

"I don't have any shields. Most Walkers don't know how to shield. There's no need, since telepathy is so rare," Nebula said.

Lyra silently watched Nebula take care of Archie. She considered trying to get through to Galena. It would be easier knowing she probably didn't have a shield. It was worth a try. She didn't mention it to Nebula or Archie in case she was unsuccessful.

Staring at Galena would give away what she was trying to do, so she pretended to rest. She leaned her head back on the chair and put her feet up.

When she first stretched her mind out, she felt Archie's familiar energy and veered away so he wouldn't suspect anything. Then she felt the uninviting fogginess Archie had explained, knowing right away it was Nebula's energy. Not physically looking at Galena proved to be a challenge. She continued searching, feeling different energies throughout the healing pod.

Finally, she practically collided with an energy surrounded by an intense light. She wasn't sure how she knew, but she knew it belonged to Galena.

Lyra stretched her mind out, pushing harder where the light shone brightest. Like she did when she communicated with Archie, she imagined a door materializing in her mind. Galena's mind had an impenetrable barrier, making it difficult for her to find a way in. Overwhelmed by exhaustion and afraid of burnout, Lyra pushed through the blinding light with a final burst of energy.

When she opened her eyes and saw Nebula standing over her, she realized she had gone too far. Lyra couldn't hear what Nebula was saying, even though her mouth was moving. Then she was gone.

Moments later, Lyra felt a cool rag against her forehead. "Easy, my beautiful star."

Lyra was about to apologize when one of Galena's guards yelled, "She's awake!"

Nebula stood. "Please, get Lyra on that bed while I take care of Galena."

In a swift motion, Lyra was lifted from the floor and carefully placed onto a bed. Although she believed being carried like a child was unnecessary, she didn't want to cause a scene while Nebula cared for Galena.

She heard Nebula. "Are you in pain? Do you want me to put you back to sleep?"

Lyra watched through a break in the curtains. Galena pinched the bridge of her nose. "No, not back to sleep. I don't want to go back to those nightmares. Yes, there's pain, but I can manage. I thought I heard Lyra, but that couldn't be right."

"You heard her. I'll get you something for the pain, then I will explain." Nebula stormed past and went straight to the counter.

Lyra sat up, feeling much better and looked to Archie. She thought she saw him trying to hide, laughing at her. *"What?"*

"Nothing. It's nothing," Archie said.

He was definitely laughing at her.

"What?"

"You should've seen the look on your face when they dumped you on the bed."

"They didn't dump *me on the bed and I didn't need to be carried. I'm fine!"*

"Hey. No need to scream. That kind of hurts."

"Oh, sorry," Lyra said. She swung her legs over the side of the bed, testing her balance. Despite feeling sore and tired, she was doing better than she had expected.

"Push me over there. I don't want to miss this," Archie said.

Lyra waved him off as she slowly made her way past the guards to check on Galena. Nebula was too busy mixing herbs and making tonics to notice.

"Hey. Sorry about that," Lyra said.

"Don't be sorry. Thank you for waking me. I couldn't stand living in those nightmares anymore. How did you do that?" Galena asked.

"Can I bring Archie closer and we can explain everything?" Lyra asked.

"Of course."

While Lyra moved Archie's bed closer, Nebula arrived with a large tray of tonics for everyone.

"I knew you wouldn't stay in bed, my beautiful star. It's been a long day." She handed Galena something for the pain, then passed around tonics, taking one for herself. "We should start from the beginning."

~Chapter 15~

Nebula had insisted on Lyra spending the night in the healing pod to receive extra tonics. Lyra gladly accepted and woke the next morning, feeling recharged.

She pulled her curtains back, heading to the wash pod. Archie walked by with a noticeable limp. "You're healing quickly," she said.

"Drink your tonics. We have work to do," he said as a way of greeting her. "While you were getting your beauty sleep, Pollux found your bracelet."

"And?"

Archie kept walking without answering her. She matched him step for step, waiting for him to say something.

"It's been examined by a team of Walker scientists. They found an element in the center they couldn't identify right away. They're doing testing right now. Pollux claims that the only way to know for sure was for someone else bend with it. Well, he's behind that curtain." Archie nodded towards a closed set of curtains.

Lyra stood frozen, flickering. "Please tell me this is a terrible joke."

"He wasn't hurt badly. He did his best to protect his particles before the bend. Nebula said it could have been much worse and he should be fine in a few days," Archie said. Lyra caught up with him again.

The doors slid open and Helix walked in.

"What's the element? Do they know how it got in there? Was it made that way?" Lyra asked.

"We don't know yet," Helix answered. He walked through the curtains hiding Pollux from view. "We suspect Saros had something to do with it, but we don't know why or how."

"We'll figure it out once I'm out of here." Lyra jumped when Archie's voice boomed through her mind. It had slipped her mind that they could have telepathic conversations.

"Can you read my thoughts?" Lyra asked.

Archie laughed. *"No, but I know you want to find out why. I'm curious, too."*

"So, it is true," Helix said. "You're both telepathic. I can't figure out how or why you guys have so many rare skills. Walkers don't have that many skills. Any idea why, Nebula?"

"I have my theories." Nebula busied herself with crushing herbs.

"Which are?" Helix joined her, helping her pour tonics into cups.

"It's too early for that. I think we will all know in time," Nebula said.

"Did you catch Janus?" Lyra asked.

"No." Helix sighed. "But I found out that he's working for Saros. I captured one of her soldiers who helped Janus escape. We will find him and make him pay for what he did to Galena."

Lyra nodded. Helix rarely showed his emotions, but she could see the determination in his eyes. This was personal. She believed he was doing everything he could to find Janus and would make him pay for what he did.

Helix went on to explaining the plans for the day. Galena, Archie, and Pollux would return to the Grotto and finish healing there. Lyra would meet everyone at the Grotto after a full day of training with Castor. They all agreed that having everyone in one place would be the safest option. Nebula had already released her other patients, so she would also stay at the Grotto.

"I feel well enough to train," Archie insisted.

Helix looked to Nebula and she nodded in agreement. "I've learned that these two don't do well sitting around the healing pod. He would be safer in the arena while I go back and forth to the Grotto preparing it for Galena and Pollux. He needs to mostly observe and not use too much energy." Then she turned to Archie, "Expect to drink tons of tonics after training. If you think you can handle that, then you can go."

"I can. Thank you," Archie said.

"Get cleaned up then bend to the training arena together. Castor will meet you there," Helix said.

Lyra was ready to leave within minutes. She tried not to hurry Archie, knowing his injury limited his mobility. As soon as he was ready, they rushed outside, excited to bend to the training area.

Castor had been waiting for them. He began with rules of safety, introducing a new rule. He declared that nobody could throw a boulder at another person until they proved they had full control.

That made Archie laugh.

"It's not funny," Lyra said, crossing her arms. She kicked a few pebbles, making them hover before letting them fall.

"They made a new rule just for you," Archie laughed harder.

"Watch it or I'll accidentally throw another boulder at you." Lyra grinned.

Castor cleared his throat. "Archer, bend to the other side of the arena. Practice holding a smaller boulder in mid-air with your mind. Once it wobbles, give your mind a rest. Nebula has you on light training, so don't push it. I will check on you once I'm done with Lyra."

Archie's particles shimmered in the sunlight before he disappeared. A second later he stood at the far end of the arena.

"Ready?" Castor asked.

Lyra wiped her sweaty hands on her clothes. It was a warm day with no wind to cool her off. Taking a deep breath, she gave a confirming nod. Without her bracelet, she knew training would be different. The magnitude of the setback bothered her considering it was caused by something so small. Not today, she thought. Today, she would train to be the Walker she was meant to be. She was ready.

"With uncertainty looming over us, we need to work on your control. I will try to distract you while you toss that boulder to that target." Castor pointed to the boulder, then to the target, a green smiley face painted on yet another boulder.

"Seriously?" She thought.

"You got this." Archie replied.

"Oh, sorry. I didn't mean to send that to you."

"I'm glad you did. You were caught off guard once and now you know to remain focused no matter what. You got this."

"Thanks." Lyra said. She took a few deep breaths while staring at the target.

"Oh, I see. Now I know what it's like for others when Lux and I have our private conversations." Castor laughed. "When I was first training, Helix said 'if you believe you can, you're halfway there.' I didn't understand him at first, but it's true. Don't talk yourself out of it. Believe in yourself."

Lyra shifted on her feet, continuing to take deep breaths. She glanced at Archie, making sure he was far away. He was still effortlessly levitating an enormous boulder and was no-where near the target.

Once she felt somewhat calmer, she levitated the boulder, immediately noticing how clear her mind felt. It took little effort to keep the boulder in the air. Oddly, it was even lighter and easier to do than last time. She focused on making the boulder spin, then changed directions and was fascinated when it responded. Then she tossed it at the target, hitting her mark with ease.

"Brilliant! That was remarkable." Castor ran towards her, smiling. "Let's play catch."

They practiced tossing a boulder back and forth while Archie rested in the shade. After a little bit, they used a bigger one until Castor was satisfied with her control. Then he left her to practice holding the boulder in the air for as long as she could while he worked with Archie.

After holding the boulder in the air for a while, Lyra felt tired and let it drop to the ground.

"Ouch."

Lyra's eyes widened in disbelief as Pollux stood next to the boulder. From where she was standing, his foot seemed trapped beneath it.

~Chapter 16~

"Just kidding," Pollux said, stepping around the boulder.

Lyra thought she'd hurt him. Even though she felt relieved to find out that it was a joke, she was angry at him for being there when he shouldn't have been. "You're supposed to be in the healing pod."

Pollux leaned against the boulder, breathing hard and he looked pale. "What she doesn't know won't hurt her." He laughed, but it seemed forced, like he was in pain.

"Go back to the healing pod. It's obvious that you're not ready to be here."

"I agree, but I have news." Pollux shifted slightly, grimacing in pain. He clasped one arm across his body, near his ribs and slid to the ground.

Castor and Archie were there in less than a second.

"What happened?" Castor asked. He bent down to check on his brother.

"Helix got a lead on your parents. Blue went with him. Nebula is with Galena in the Grotto, so I had time to break free before she noticed."

"A lead is not worth risking your health. You look awful. Go back to the healing pod," Lyra snapped.

"As long as I don't move too much, I'll be fine. This is a nice spot to rest."

Castor rolled his eyes. "I'll be back." Then he disappeared, leaving the slightest shimmer before completely disappearing.

"I forgot to tell you happy birthday. Time is strange here. Sorry. Anyway, happy birthday!"

"Oh, thanks. That was random," she laughed.

"Happy Earth birthday," Pollux grinned.

"Thanks."

"Hold out your hand," Archie said.

Archie removed a tiny ball, similar in size to a dime, from his pocket and placed it in her hand. She glanced downward and observed its light shade, resembling a perfectly baked golden-brown cookie. Curiosity filled her eyes as she glanced at him.

"It's called a starburst. Not like the candy we have on Earth, but it's good. Slowly bite down on it for the full effect." Archie smiled, showing off his dimple.

By biting down on it, Lyra made it burst open, filling her senses with a delightfully cool and minty sensation. The flavor quickly transformed into a sweet strawberry as she continued chewing. "Wow. I get why it's called a starburst."

"I have a few more. Different ones." Archie held his hand out, offering one to Lyra and Pollux. "It's not gum, but it lasts longer than a starburst."

"Thanks," Pollux said. "I haven't had one of these in a while. How did you get your hands on them?"

"I asked Nebula to help find something for Lyra's birthday. She said these come from another planet."

When Lyra tried it, she found the texture to be hard and unbreakable. "It's like chewing on an eraser. I can't break it. Are you sure this is candy?"

"They soften up, then open. That's when the fun starts," Pollux said. "Sorry, we missed your birthday, Lyra. Walkers don't celebrate birthdays like Earth people do. We don't age the same."

Castor materialized where he had disappeared moments ago. "Drink these if you are going to be stubborn and stay here." He gave Pollux a few tonics and placed a pillow behind him.

Pollux smiled and sipped the first tonic while chewing the candy.

"Does that mean Archie and I won't age like normal Earth people?" Lyra asked.

Archie offered some candy to Castor. Castor took a piece and nodded.

"You'll live for thousands of years and not look a day over twenty Earth years," Pollux said.

"Why?" Lyra and Archie said.

"Once the mind is awakened, strange things happen. Walkers don't talk about their age often. Lux and I look like we're about 15 years old on Earth, but we're actually 4,485 cosmic years."

"That sounds like a lot, but what are cosmic years compared to Earth years? They can't be light years because those aren't actually years? It's the distance light travels in a year. That would make you 90 trillion miles old." Archie mused.

Castor took a seat next to Pollux, motioning for Lyra and Archie to take a seat on the ground as well. "Time is different on each planet. Earth people measure time in seconds, minutes, days, weeks, months, and years. Time is different on Alora. Walkers created cosmic years to make it less confusing. It's a universal formula to figure out a comparable age while on another planet."

"How old would Archie and I be in cosmic years?" Lyra asked.

"Three thousand, five hundred, eighty-eight cosmic years," Archie said.

Lyra laughed. Of course, Archie would've figured it out already.

"I don't sound so old now, do I? Pollux winked at Lyra.

A blush spread across her face, matching the butterflies in her stomach. She didn't want to admit that she had a crush on Pollux. He was funny with a carefree attitude, and those green eyes seemed to lock with hers way too often. No, she would have to think about all of that later. Things were already complicated enough. She didn't want to add that into the mix.

"Well, I think we should get back to training." Lyra stood, brushing the dirt off of her clothes.

"Lyra, there's something I want you to try. First, we'll meditate. That will help you focus your energy on separating your mind from our body," Castor suggested.

"Why would I want to do that?" Lyra asked.

"I have a theory. Are you willing to try?" Castor asked.

"Sure, why not?"

"Good. Come with me." Castor walked further away from where Pollux and Archie were resting.

Lyra found it challenging to contain her amusement as Castor settled into a meditation position on the ground. Something caught her eye in the sky. "That's the weirdest cloud. It's moving like a…bird?"

"That's a stratalatus. Good eye. Okay, are you ready? Sit." He patted the ground next to him. "Good. Take a slow breath through your nose and hold it. Exhale through your mouth. You're going to distance your mind energy from your physical energy. This exercise will help you access your skills faster, bend faster, and protect yourself quicker. Reach out and make sure you can feel every part of your body with your mind. Got it?"

"Yup," Lyra said.

"Good. Now imagine pulling your mind away from your physical being, like you're hovering above your body. Maybe you're a balloon or just a bubble floating above. How would you see yourself if you could look down at yourself? How would your hair look if you were two feet above your body? Now three feet above…four feet. Look at the arena as you hover over your body. Can you see where I am sitting? Can you see Pollux and Archie?"

Castor waited a few seconds before asking, "Were you able to pull your mind away, Lyra?"

His voice sounded like it was getting further away—much further away.

Lyra couldn't see herself from above when she opened her eyes. She saw Castor, Pollux, and

Archie, but not herself. When she opened her mouth to answer Castor's question, nothing came out. Everyone grew smaller and smaller until she couldn't see them. She wondered if her body had gone invisible because nothing else made sense.

A slight movement caught her attention. She refocused and saw Castor and Archie waving their arms. Pollux stood near them. Her anger dissipated and turned into fear as she realized she was too high and far from the ground. She had no idea how to get back to her body. Floating higher once more, she lost sight of them completely.

Following a moment of panic, she calmed herself by taking deep breaths and clearing her worries. In order to stop herself from floating even higher, she imagined sinking slowly to the ground. Like a hot air balloon, she opened the imaginary vent, letting out heat and slowly descending to the ground. The twins' and Archie's voice grew louder as she drew closer.

The ground was getting closer at an alarming speed. She extended her hand to prepare for landing, suddenly aware that she could see it. She looked around, inspecting her body. Realization hit hard, and her heart raced with panic. She hadn't separated her body from her mind. Instead, she'd levitated herself, just as she had done with the boulder, and now she was plummeting towards the ground.

She closed her eyes, feeling the rush of wind against her face as she braced for the inevitable collision with the ground. She knew it would hurt

and she would probably end up in the healing pod—
again.

~Chapter 17~

"Gotcha," Pollux yelped in pain as he caught her.

Lyra was thankful for not getting hurt but furious at him for risking his safety to catch her.

"You idiot! Put me down." Despite his pain, she broke free from his hold. She noticed confusion on his face.

"A thank you would be nice." Pollux grimaced, clutching his side.

"You should be in the healing pod instead of hurting yourself even more. I can't believe you did that."

Pollux waved her off. "I couldn't let you fall to the ground. I'm fine."

"You look awful," Lyra said as he swayed off balance.

She went to grab him, but Castor beat her to it. He grabbed Pollux around the waist, supporting him. "You shouldn't have done that. Archie and I were prepared to catch her."

"Sure, sure. But Lyra? How did you do *that?* I've never seen anyone levitate," Pollux said.

Lyra took Pollux's free arm and hung it around her neck. Castor silently nodded his thanks for her help.

"I didn't think I was still connected to my physical being until I fell towards the ground, then I panicked. I'm sorry for hurting you." She sniffled, unable to wipe her tears away.

"I'm not any worse than I was before. I couldn't—I wouldn't let you get hurt again. I'll be fine," Pollux said through gritted teeth. "I want to see you do that again."

"Me too," Archie admitted.

"Do you think you can?" Castor asked.

"You guys are crazy. He needs to get back to the healing pod," Lyra demanded.

"I have another theory. Lux, you good to hang out for a little longer?" Castor asked.

"Sure thing," Pollux said. He removed his arm from Lyra and let Castor lower him to the ground.

Lyra shook her head. "You guys really are crazy." She didn't think she could do that again. She wasn't even sure how she did it the first time.

Castor walked closer and whispered, "Do you still have trouble with reading?"

The question caught her off guard. "What?"

"Walkers can levitate objects, but we can't levitate another person, especially not ourselves. The way your mind works is absolutely amazing."

"Um…no. My mind is the reason I struggle in school and probably why I couldn't do what you wanted me to do," she argued.

"It depends on how you choose to look at it. Will you try something?"

Lyra hesitated, uncertain about attempting anything else. She was convinced she would mess up again. She glanced over at Pollux, making sure he was alright. He gave a smile that was filled with encouragement. She looked at Archie and he smiled back at her. She believed that if they had faith in her, she should give it a shot.

"If this doesn't work, we're done for the day and Pollux goes back to the healing pod. Deal?" Lyra said.

They all nodded.

Castor motioned for her to follow him. When they'd walked a short distance, he gestured for her to sit. Then he walked a little further before sitting on the ground. Lyra took a seat where he'd left her and let out a frustrated sigh.

"This time, toss your mind away from your physical being, just like you're tossing a boulder to Archie." Castor waved Archie over. "Stand over there and be ready to catch."

"On it." Archie's particles shimmered for a second before he reappeared where Castor wanted him to be.

"You want me to toss my mind to Archie? Do you know how weird that sounds?"

Castor grinned while nodding.

"You got this," Archie said.

Lyra could see why Castor suggested it and thought that maybe it would work. "Okay. I'll try it."

"Ready when you are," Archie said to her. His hands were held out in front of him, ready to catch whatever came his way.

Lyra took a deep breath. "I can do this," she mumbled to herself. She closed her eyes and repeated those words. When trying to separate her energies wasn't working, she pulled back to reset before trying again. She tried repeatedly.

"Lyra, you're flickering in and out of sight," Castor said.

"Please help?" she begged Archie.

"I think you're trying too hard. It's more of a feeling that can't be forced. Breathe, relax, and let it happen. You got this," Archie said to her.

She knew he was right, and she had been trying really hard to make it happen. This time when she extended her mind, she let her energies guide her. Then it hit her. She was thinking about her mental and physical energies as things, but what they actually do. Maybe she could separate them if she gave them something to do, she thought. She commanded her physical energy to maintain a stable heart rate while breathing.

Once she focused her physical energy, she tried pulling her mental energy away. The process proved to be challenging, forcing her to tap into her reserves. Every time it felt like she was close, her physical energy yanked her back with the force of a neodymium magnet.

It wasn't working.

Lyra took a deep breath, realizing she had been going about this all wrong. Separating the two energies had nothing to do with the energies themselves; it was all about the process. In order to understand what set them apart, she had to understand their connection.

Hoping she'd figured it out, Lyra entered a deep state of meditation with little effort. She cast her thoughts out, allowing them to guide her. Soon enough, she was led to an unfamiliar place that demanded her attention. She found herself encircled by a kaleidoscope of colors. She was tempted to reach out and touch them. Fearing it would break her concentration, she resisted. Instead, she let herself gravitate towards the most dynamic color, instantly recognizing it as her mental energy. Then there was a muted color she recognized as her physical energy. She focused on grounding her physical energy in place.

With her physical energy anchored down, she focused on the other color, which was incredibly bright. It reminded her of the feeling just before bending with its cold, prickly edges. She wondered how something so bright could feel so uninviting.

Instead of pulling on her mental energy, she imagined making it into a ball that she could throw to Archie. Without warning, she heard a loud snap and was jolted backward. She succeeded.

It was an odd feeling, like she was exposed and vulnerable. Instinctively, she twirled her mental energy into a tightly protected orb, then hurled it away from her body towards Archie.

Surprisingly, she didn't feel the impact but heard Archie yell, "What. Was. That?"

Lyra questioned whether she had made a mistake when it felt so perfect. She focused on pulling her mental energy back towards her physical body. Knowing what to look for, she effortlessly found the connection and merged the energies together again.

She opened her eyes to find Archie hunched over with his hands on his knees as he took in gulps of air. She'd obviously knocked the wind out of him, but hadn't hurt him.

Feeling confident that she could do it quicker this time, she said. "I'm going to try that again. Ready?"

He held up his hand. "Wait." Then he laughed. He was still hunched over, but he was laughing.

Pollux's laughter echoed across the arena. "If I were you, I would take a stronger stance. Maybe wear a helmet. Or some kind of armor."

Archie positioned himself defensively, with one foot behind him and his hands raised, prepared to withstand the impact. "Ready."

"This is amazing," Castor said.

The process was quicker since she knew what to do. Lyra spun her mental energy into an orb, feeling calmer and in more control. She gently tossed it to Archie.

A few minutes passed before anyone spoke. "Lyra? Are you ok?" Castor asked.

"Lyra?" Pollux asked when she hadn't responded to Castor. She couldn't respond, not when her body wasn't connected to her mental energy.

"She's right here." Archie held his arms, as if cradling a baby. "It feels like the same energy from when she knocked the air out of my lungs. She has considerable control." He sounded surprised, maybe even impressed.

Lyra gently pulled her orb of mental energy back towards her physical being. This time, the energies snapped back together on their own. She spoke as soon as she could. "My energies feel more connected now that I can separate them. If that makes any sense."

"It makes perfect sense. Bending, levitation, separating your energies and using your skills are very complex. The more you practice, the easier it becomes." Castor walked towards Pollux, motioning for Archie and Lyra to join them.

"Quantum theory of relativity?" Archie asked as soon as they were all standing around Pollux.

"You would make Einstein very proud," Pollux laughed. Archie gave him a hard look.

"Quantum theory of what?" Lyra was familiar with the words, but couldn't remember what it meant.

"The Theory of Relativity or simply the largest things, like the universe. Then there's quantum physics, or the smallest things, like particles, atoms, neutrons, protons, and electrons. Since we are dealing with both and defining the laws of nature, wouldn't it be the Quantum Theory of Relativity?" With arms crossed and a huge grin, Archie looked proud of himself.

"Isn't that an oxymoron?" Lyra didn't quite understand.

"Yes, it would be, but Archie is onto something. What about the Quantum Theory of Gravity, since we are defying the laws of gravity as well?" Castor suggested.

"That's a good one." Archie agreed.

"You two nerds can talk theory over dinner. I think we should call it a day and get back to the healing pod. Lyra, are you ready?" Pollux asked.

"Ready? For what?"

"To help me bend back to the healing pod." Pollux grinned, making Lyra's cheeks flush.

"Lux, I'll take you back. Lyra's got impressive control, especially after today's training, but she's too exhausted to bend while protecting someone else." Castor helped pull Pollux to his feet. "You two go to the Grotto. I'll meet you there after I get Pollux settled."

"Party pooper," Pollux mumbled. A playful grin spread across his face.

Lyra nodded, then said to Archie, "*See you at the Grotto.*"

In fear of blushing again, she refused to look at Pollux before closing her eyes. She focused on where she wanted to go, feeling the familiar prickly coolness as her body prepared for the bend. The image of the Grotto quickly changed into an image of a strange place she'd never seen before. It was too late for her to stop the bend. The new image became a reality. She spotted a familiar face, his lips forming a mischievous smile.

"Janus," she snarled.

~Chapter 18~

"It worked," Janus sneered. "Where's the boy?"

He was there for moment, then disappeared.

Lyra slowly turned in circles, desperately looking for him. She wanted to know where he was in case, he attacked her. The tall, dense trees and shrubs blocked her view. It looked like she had traveled back to prehistoric times. The leaves on the trees were twice her size, making her feel tiny like an ant on Earth.

Her palms were sweaty and her heart pounded so fast that she felt it in her throat. She opened her mouth, but no sound came out. She didn't know how she got there, but she knew Janus had somehow hijacked her bend and sent her here. She had to find her way back to Alora.

"Do not bend. Remember what happened when you had your bracelet on?" Janus warned. "Where do you think we got that element from? You are surrounded by it. You will not make it out alive." He released a deep and threatening laugh, causing a shiver to run down her back.

Lyra swallowed hard. She had to distract him. "No one needs to get hurt. Can we just talk?"

"You're on a strange planet. You can't bend out of here and no one knows where you are, but you want to talk? What a strange request. What could you possibly have to talk about?" His voice grew softer, tinged with a sense of curiosity.

"How did I end up here?" Lyra waited, hoping to use the diversion to trace his voice, but when he talked, it seemed to echo everywhere.

"That's my little secret." He laughed. "No more wasting my time. Now, you will cooperate if you want to see your family—alive. I'm sure you can predict how this will end if you don't."

Lyra's fists tightened at her sides. "And how will it end if I don't cooperate?" It was then that she noticed him. Had he lied, she wondered. He could bend without getting hurt. She looked around him, trying to find anything that would mark where he stood, about fifty feet away from her.

He was facing her, partially hiding behind a large leaf. Even though she was far away, she spotted minor cuts and bruises on his face, yet it was possible they were merely shadows caused by the trees and leaves surrounding him.

"If your face looks like that, I hope the rest of you is even worse. I'm glad to see that Galena wasn't the only one hurt," she said.

"My sister was trained well. That is true. But you—you haven't had more than what—a few days' worth of training? You are no match, even at my weakest," Janus snorted.

"You have no right to call her your sister. A *brother* wouldn't attack his sister and leave her to die. You're a coward," Lyra spat. She took a few deep breaths, calming herself before speaking again. "Let me go or this will only end badly for *you*."

"You have no idea who or what you're dealing with," Janus growled.

"I am not alone." Remembering her lifeline, she pressed the buttons with increasing urgency.

"Your arrogance is refreshing. We both know there's no one else here. Enough talking. It's simple. You can come with me in one piece or in pieces. The choice is yours." Janus whistled a long, eerie tune.

The ground trembled with intense vibrations, causing Lyra to lose her balance. She immediately lowered into a fighting stance to regain her balance. She found it difficult to control her panic and calm her racing heart as she watched the oversized trees fall like dominos.

Janus caught her gaze, and for a moment, their eyes were locked before his smile grew wider. She realized she was exactly where he wanted her to be. If she couldn't escape, she would be trapped.

The violent shaking of the ground made it impossible for her to run without losing her balance. Like a guppy caught on a fishing hook, she had no choice but to wait. In desperation, she repeatedly pressed her lifeline.

Janus, clearly not worried about her escaping, turned to confront whatever he had summoned. As the dust and debris cleared, Lyra got a glimpse of something enormous with a grayish, scaly skin. Trees were flattened beneath its massive feet, crushed by the force of its weight. The word "monstrous" couldn't fully capture the enormity of what stood behind Janus.

Janus stretched his arms outward and whistled a high-pitched melody. The creature obeyed, gently lifting him off the ground with one of its two trunks. It smoothly swung Janus onto the back of its neck where a saddle-like apparatus was secured.

It was taller than any building Lyra had seen. Pointy spikes, starting below its eyes, ran down to the middle of each of its two trunks. Adding to its defense, it had three large and sharp tusks. Its gray scales shimmered like a rainbow as it breathed. Lyra noticed its underbelly had a wrinkly grayish skin, similar to that of an elephant from Earth.

The creature stepped forward slightly, gaining ground. Lyra grabbed hold of a nearby branch to steady herself. Janus whistled again, and it took a step back again. She wondered why the creature obeyed him and how Janus had gained control over something so powerful and deadly.

"Oh, don't hide now, Lyra. We're just getting started," Janus sneered. He scanned the area.

Realizing she'd become invisible; she used it to her advantage to buy her more time to come up with a plan. There had to be a way to bend off the planet. If not, then Janus had to be trapped, but she knew he wouldn't do that to himself. He had to have a way to deliver her to Saros.

"Come out so I can see you. I know you're here—hiding." Janus continued to look around.

She didn't try to bend, especially if Janus was telling the truth. She spotted the trees that were shaped like a cat then looked for the leaves with small holes in them. That's where she'd seen him bend earlier and it was her best bet to get off the planet. She had to try.

Fearful that the creature would hear her, she waited to make her move. There was silence, except for the wind softly whistling through leaves and shrubs. She knew it was only a matter of time before Janus would inevitably say something. Then she would gain a few steps closer to safety.

"I know you're still here. I can feel your potential—your energy. You're much stronger than last time. Yes, much stronger indeed. Saros will be pleased," he mused.

Lyra gained a little ground. She hoped Janus wouldn't grow tired of talking to himself. This was the best plan she had. She crept a little closer to where she wanted to go, all the while watching Janus and the creature intently.

"Did they tell you about Saros? I'm certain my dear sister let you in on all the secrets by now." He laughed. "Little do you know the game she plays. You're being kept in the dark, Lyra. With the potential you have, you could truly help the cause." He squinted his eyes, looking right past her.

She moved cautiously, not wanting to give her location away with a crunch of a leaf. But when Janus paused, she became motionless.

"Ever wonder why Alora doesn't have advanced technology?" He said, flashing another smug grin. "Let me tell you, it's not because they don't have the ability or the means. Oh, no, not at all. It's because my father believed in keeping his people in the dark. If you only knew Master's secrets." His gaze shifted from left to right, scanning his surroundings. He clearly looked irritated when he couldn't find her.

Lyra doubted she could reach the spot in time before Janus became impatient. She desperately pressed her lifelines, knowing it was a long shot. She considered making a run for it. The creature would certainly hear her, and Janus would have her flattened before she could bend. She waited for him to talk again.

"What happens if you keep people in the dark, you ask?" Janus sighed. "They become weak. You know someone like this, don't you?"

Lyra lost count of the number of times she'd pressed the lifelines. She wondered if the deadly element affected them, too. She was curious who he was blabbering about, but knew he would soon say.

"Nebula's lost everything. Her family, her friends, her home planet. She came to Alora broken. She's wasting her true potential hiding there. She chose to be in the dark, but what do you gain from it? You're actually being held captive. Did you realize that yet? They know where your family is, but give you excuses for why they haven't been rescued. Let me make it clear. You're on the wrong side, Lyra. Saros is offering you so much more. You can be with your family again. Don't you want to know how they're doing?" Janus looked smug, sitting tall in his seat.

Lyra knew he was taunting her, hoping for a reaction. She dropped her invisibility. "Of course, I want to know how my family is doing, but I highly doubt you'll tell me."

"There you are. Clever. How did you do that? A trick of the light?"

"If Saros wants Archie and I on her side, why did she take my family? Did she hurt them? Where are they?" Lyra's voice cracked. She didn't care if he saw her cry. She desperately wanted to hear that her family was safe and unharmed.

"Tut-tut, Miss Lyra. The truth is to be earned."

"Truth? You twist the truth for your own benefit. You don't know who or what you are dealing with. We all have this skill. I'm not alone."

"You're a pathetic liar. I can sense that you're alone."

"Just tell me where my family is—" Lyra went invisible again. She knew she wouldn't get answers from him.

"They're safe, for now." He smirked. "It's funny how you assume these wounds are from Galena. Saros doesn't take kindly to those who fail her. I will not fail again. Invisible or not, I will bring you to her." He whistled a strange melody.

The creature responded. It lifted its trunks high and let out a low, prolonged sound from one trunk, while the other produced a high-pitched tone.

The bone-shaking mix of highs and lows made it impossible to concentrate. Lyra's hands flew to her ears. The ground trembled beneath her feet, threatening to knock her off balance once more. Steadying herself against a tree trunk, she pressed all the lifelines simultaneously.

She wouldn't make it easy for Janus if these were her last moments. She needed a distraction.

"You coward!" she shouted.

"Enough! Either you die now or come willingly. It's your choice," Janus said.

"I will never go with you," she shouted.

"Don't be a fool. Come with me and your family will be safe or choose death for yourself and your family."

His words rattled her, but she kept quiet. If he couldn't see her or hear her, his creatures would have a harder time finding her. As she waited, she saw two more elephant-like creatures materialize beside Janus' creature. The creatures stomped their feet, causing the ground to shake again. Lyra gained a few steps.

Within minutes, Janus had somehow calmed the creatures. All three stood tall and proud, like statues.

Lyra wondered how Janus controlled them.

"With one whistle, the elpinitida will flatten the area, including you, within seconds. You cannot escape. So, what will it be?"

Lyra stood mere feet away from the spot, her body tingling with a mix of excitement and nervousness. She considered making a run for it and taking her chances with being squashed by those massive creatures.

"I'll take your silence as your answer." Janus licked his lips, then formed an 'o' with his mouth.

Lyra stared at him, unable to move. She should say something, but no words came out when she opened her mouth. She knew these were her last moments.

"Maybe she's been stalling you." Helix materialized about ten feet from Lyra. He winked at her as she flickered in and out of sight.

Tears brimmed her eyes, as a wave of relief washed over her. She couldn't believe Helix had found her in the nick of time. Alongside Helix, stood Blue, Castor, and Archie in fighting stances, all focused on Janus.

"Janus was just saying how the elpinitida will flatten this entire area within seconds," Lyra said. She wanted to warn them without letting Janus know how afraid she was for everyone's safety.

"They are capable of doing just that with the correct commands." Helix's nostrils flared as he bared his teeth at Janus in warning.

"Yes, you would know. You would also know that when elpinitida are present, so are gigantius, or ogres to you. Meet Orcus and Pluto," Janus sneered. With a dismissive wave of his hand towards Helix, he began whistling an unusual melody.

Two massive, almost humanoid figures emerged slowly from behind the towering trees. Lyra immediately noticed one had only a single eye positioned in the center of its forehead, while the other had two little beady eyes. They stared at her and her friends with an unsettling intensity. With drool seeping from their mouths, they snarled like a rabid animal. The muscles on their bare chests rippled with sheer power as they breathed. Luckily, they had loincloths crafted from big leaves secured by vines while their bare feet were covered in dirt and grime.

A pungent stench drifted her way, making her gag. These creatures desperately needed a bath and clean clothes. Lyra giggled, imaging them brushing their disgustingly yellow teeth with an oversized toothbrush.

"Something funny?" Janus asked.

"You're sitting on oversized elephants with a cyclops and its sidekick standing guard next to you. What? You can't beat a sixth-grader on your own? All of this," Lyra, now visible, waved her hand at the creatures, "makes you look weak." Lyra laughed.

"Careful," Helix warned her.

"I would listen to him. He doesn't want to lose another loved one, does he?" Janus mocked.

Helix's primitive growl echoed through the air. The cyclops responded with deep, menacing growl of its own. Helix held his stance, refusing to look away from Janus.

Lyra wanted to know what Janus meant about Helix losing a loved one, but she knew it wasn't the right time to ask.

"We can't bend out of here," Lyra directed her thoughts towards Archie, Blue, Castor, and Helix. *"That deadly rare element is here, all around us. Saros must have switched my bracelet at some point. I don't know how Janus got me here, but if we bend, we won't live. I am a few feet away from where Janus was earlier and I think it's safe to bend from there."*

"Together," Helix mouthed.

"Bend together?" Lyra clarified.

Helix and Blue nodded, reaching out their hands.

"We have to get to that spot first. It's our best bet." Lyra suggested.

Janus didn't waste time. He let out a series of commands as Lyra ran to the spot, quickly turning around towards her friends. She watched them lose their balance as the ground trembled and shook. Trees crashed to the ground, but they kept running and she held her hands out towards them. She knew it would be a matter of seconds before they were captured or squashed by the monstrous creatures.

Once everyone made it, they gripped each other tightly, mixing their energies. "To the healing pod," Helix yelled. Lyra wrapped her mind around her particles, feeling the coldness rip them away.

~Chapter 19~

"What happened?" Helix yelled. His hands were on his hips as he stood in front of her.

Lyra reached her breaking point and couldn't hold back the tears any longer. She dropped to the ground with her face buried in her palms and she let the tears flow to the ground. She couldn't handle being yelled at, especially after she thought those monstrous creatures were going to flatten her or she would be captured and brought to Saros.

Nebula stood near her with a hand on her shoulder. "You really scared us." Then she pulled Lyra to her feet and hugged her. "Let's get you to a chair."

After Nebula looked her over with her gadget, she moved onto Archie. Helix stood nearby, obviously waiting for a response.

"I was getting ready to bend to the Grotto when my vision shifted to that planet. I tried to stop the bend, but I couldn't. I don't know how it happened," Lyra admitted.

"That's impossible." Helix's arms dropped to his sides.

"I've been getting these faint glimpses of places I don't recognize before I bend as well. I didn't know it was of that place until we were there. How did he do it? It's like he hijacked our minds," Archie asked. Nebula finished with him and moved onto Helix, but he waved her away.

"Impossible," Helix repeated, his face pinched in deep thought. "Sorry, Nebula. I'm fine though."

Nebula nodded, then handed out tonics to everyone. It reminded Lyra of how her mom always took care of everyone. She thanked Nebula before taking a sip of the light greenish tonic, which was bitter-tasting.

Archie asked her, "Are you okay?"

"Yeah, I'm fine." Lyra smiled, hoping he would believe her.

Helix stopped pacing and sat in an empty chair. "Did Janus tell you anything about your family?"

"He said that Archie and I are on the wrong side and don't know the truth. He said I was wasting my potential. Oh, and Saros gave him those wounds, not Galena," Lyra said. "How did you find me?"

"By pressing the lifelines multiple times, we were able to track you," Blue said, placing his empty glass on the counter near Nebula. Lyra thought she saw him mouth a thank you to Nebula and wondered if something more was going on between those two.

"Did he mention anything else?" Helix asked.

Lyra sat back, thinking about everything Janus said. Helix tapped his fingers on the arm of the chair, distracting her thoughts. "Can you stop that? Please?"

"Janus loves to talk and sometimes gives hints away. What else did he say?" Helix asked.

"I wasn't paying attention to everything he said. I was trying to distract him so I could bend. Can you please stop tapping? I can't think." Lyra snapped.

Helix stopped. "I didn't realize. Sorry. Please tell me everything. This is important."

"He wouldn't tell me how I ended up there and he was shocked that Archie wasn't with me. He didn't say much about my family or anything else. He gave me a choice, to go with him or die. I was too focused on escaping to remember anything else."

Helix hoisted himself out of the chair. "Castor, go to Galena and let her know what happened. I'll return in a day or two. Until then, Blue you are to stay with Lyra and Archie. Either walk them to the Grotto or remain here. They are not to bend because it might be harder to find them next time."

Helix was gone before Blue could say anything. Blue sighed. "I hate when he does that."

"How can we save our families now?" Lyra cried.

"This is a slight setback. Helix is Galena's Defense Commander. He has a team of skilled Walkers to help figure this out. We have Walkers working on rescuing your families. These things take time. We'll figure this out." Nebula said.

Lyra nodded, although she wasn't sure she believed a word of it. This wasn't a minor setback, it was astronomical. She needed a new plan.

"We should leave for the Grotto before it gets too dark. Night fall is when creatures venture out of the Blaze and the Froid. We could do without any more adventures for the day." Blue's smile did not reach his eyes. "First, I need to speak with Lyra." He gestured for her to follow him outside.

Lyra wondered if she had done something wrong. Her stomach felt nauseous and her palms sweating. She took a few deep breaths, then followed him outside.

Right before the metal doors sealed shut behind her, she heard Archie's voice in her head, *"Tell me everything."*

"Helix found out something and there's debate if we should tell you guys. Nebula and I agree you should know. However, we're not sure how to tell Archie. We thought it would be best if the news comes from you," Blue said.

Lyra's knees buckled under her. Blue caught her before she fell to the ground. "No, no, no," she cried.

"Hey, it's not what you think it is. Your family is safe."

"Archie's dad?" Lyra forced out.

"Safe. He's safe too."

Taking a deep breath, Lyra blinked her tears away. With all her strength, she struck Blue with a backhanded blow to the chest. He staggered back a few steps. "Never, ever, do that again. You scared me," Lyra yelled.

"Ouch," Blue rubbed the spot where he'd been struck. "Well, the news I have to tell you won't be much better."

"What is it?" Lyra reached for her bracelet only to remember it was gone.

Blue walked closer to her then whispered, "We recently confirmed Saros's real identity. Her Earth name is Sarah. She's Archer's mom."

"What do you mean, *confirmed?*" She couldn't have heard him correctly. There was no way that Saros could be Archie's mom. He had already lost her once, and it nearly ripped him apart. If he knew she was alive and she was Saros, —the evilest person in the universe, it would destroy him all over again.

She appreciated that Blue stood silent, giving her a moment to digest the information.

"She faked her death?" Lyra asked. It was a rhetorical question. She knew Blue would have double-checked before sharing this with her.

Blue nodded.

"How are you going to tell him?"

"It would be better coming from you. He trusts you the most," Blue said.

"I can't—"

"You're his best friend." Blue cut in. "Can you imagine what it would do to him coming from anyone else?"

"It will destroy him either way. You have to know that." Lyra threw her hands up in the air. "We can't do this to him."

"He's going to find out. The sooner he knows, the better. Saros could be planning to shock him with the truth to win him back. We cannot lose him to her. That's what she wants. Listen, it's a long walk to the Grotto. Think about it. I'm sorry to put this on you. I am, but I would want my best friend to break the news to me."

Lyra dried her face with the back of her sleeve. "I'll think about it."

As soon as they walked into the healing pod, Archie said, "What's wrong?"

Lyra looked at Blue. He gave her a reassuring nod. "I'll tell you on the way."

"Tell me now," Archie's voice boomed in her head, making her headache worse.

She grabbed her head. "Head hurts. Please, don't. I need a few minutes to think."

"We need to go," Blue warned. "Meet us as soon as you're released." Blue smiled at Pollux.

"You got it, boss," Pollux said, winking at Lyra. She returned a half smile before following Blue and Archie outside.

The walk to the Grotto felt endless. At first, Archie gave her the space she needed to sort through her thoughts. After a while, he begged her to tell him what was going on. She agreed she should be the one to break the news to him. She would want him to do the same for her. She just didn't want to hurt him.

"Are you sure you want to know? Once I tell you this, I can't undo it." Lyra bit her lip, hoping he would consider her words. It was the best warning she could give him.

"Tell me." Archie grabbed her arm, making her stop and face him. He stared into her eyes. "I can sense this is going to suck, but I want to know."

There was no gentle way to tell him. Throughout the entire walk, she agonized over how to phrase it, but nothing could have prepared her for this moment. After a long pause, she finally mustered the words, "Your mom is still alive."

~Chapter 20~

Archie's hand fell to his side. All he did was stare at her, refusing to say anything.

"There's more."

They stood only a few feet from the Grotto's entrance. Lyra looked at Blue, who encouraged her to continue. "Your mom, well, she's actually Saros. I'm so sorry." Lyra hesitantly stepped back, giving Archie space.

After a few moments of silence, Archie asked. "Why does it *feel* like you're telling the truth?"

"Because this is the truth. We only recently found out," Blue said.

Lyra felt Blue's hand on her shoulder. "Breathe. You're flickering." The air felt thin and suffocating.

Archie balled his hands into fists, then punched the wall.

Lyra flinched. She wanted to say something, but the words caught in her throat. Nothing could make this easier.

Blue motioned for them to follow. "Inside. It's getting dark. It's not safe out here."

Archie only nodded, then walked past Lyra into the Grotto. Blue led them to a pod furnished with a table and chairs. Archie sat down and, with an unexpected calmness, he said, "The timing doesn't make sense. My mom passed away years ago."

"Yes, Earth years. We assumed she had perished with her father, Alectryon during the final battle. Instead, she led us to believe she was dead and fled to Earth. We know now that she made a life for herself as Sarah," Blue said, watching Archie for a reaction.

"The timing?" Archie repeated.

"Time moves slower on some planets and faster on others, which makes timelines confusing and unreliable. The truth is that Sarah is Saros and Saros is Sarah." Blue took a seat across from Archie.

"Why would she put me through that? Why fake her death, abandon her family just to capture me later? It doesn't make sense," Archie said. His knuckles were turning white and he was shaking.

"I don't think she thought it would be difficult to get you back. Archer, you're shaking. If you bend, you could end up somewhere worse than where Janus took Lyra. They will be more prepared this time. Breathe slowly, please. You too, Lyra. You're flickering." Blue's face was filled with concern.

In a panic, Lyra pressed her lifeline to Nebula.

Archie opened and closed his mouth repeatedly, but no sound came out. Lyra was pretty sure Archie was in shock. She felt like telling him about his mom was a mistake.

Nebula practically ran into the pod, trailed by Pollux. Lyra was surprised to see Pollux walking normally in such a short amount of time.

"He knows?" Nebula asked, but didn't wait for an answer as she opened a big bag, pulling out her gadget.

"This was a mistake." Lyra stood, only to come face-to-face with Pollux. His arms were crossed. He didn't say a word, only winking at Lyra when their eyes met. "Let me guess. You're here to be *my* distraction? It won't work. You knew, she knew, and you let me tell him. Look at him. Are you happy?"

"It's not like that," Pollux started, but Lyra pushed past him, feeling a little guilty when she heard him groan in pain. She realized he hadn't miraculously healed. She was too angry to offer an apology.

Without being able to bend anywhere or even leave the Grotto, she leaned against a wall in the far corner watching as Nebula tended to Archie. Archie drank down whatever Nebula handed in then immediately slumped forward. Nebula waved for Blue and Pollux to help her. With Blue by her side, they supported Archie, pulling him to his feet. He wasn't completely passed out. Whatever she had given him made him so relaxed that they were able to guide him away from the table.

"What did you give him? Where are you taking him?" Lyra step closer to them, but Pollux stopped her, placing his hand on her arm. She immediately felt a surge of energy and quickly pulled away from him. "Did you feel that?" She gasped.

"Feel what?" Pollux studied her face. "You could use some rest, too. Before you argue, I want you to know that I am not here to distract you. I am here to watch him. He'll rest while I finish healing. They gave him something to help him sleep. That's all."

Lyra looked at them and knew they wouldn't hurt him. She nodded then stepped out of their way.

"I can help." Pollux took Nebula's place, supporting Archie. Lyra watched as they dragged him out of the pod.

Nebula stayed behind. "Are you okay?"

"How is Pollux basically healed already?" Lyra asked, avoiding the question.

"I gave him something to mask the pain but not heal. He will stay with Archie tonight. Are you okay?"

"Not really. I've never seen Archie like that. I'm worried about him." Lyra wrapped her arms around herself, feeling even more lonely than ever.

"He just needs time. I'm afraid I can't stay. My stems need to be revitalized and I too, need rest. It's been a long day for all of us," Nebula said.

"How do you revitalize?"

"I have an artificial sunlight machine. Master gave it to me years ago for staying on Alora as their healer. Since the pods don't get enough sunlight, the machine provides my body with what it needs to survive."

"I keep forgetting you are literally a living plant by Earth standards."

"Just like you. We are not so different. We might look a little different, but we are made from the same elements and require similar needs to stay alive. Our hearts beat the same, we breathe the same and we feel emotions and pain all the same."

"Wow. That's pretty cool. Too bad people on Earth think aliens from outer space look very different. They would flip if they knew the truth." Lyra was thankful for the change of subject. She really wanted to be with Archie, but knew there was nothing she could do for him.

"I'm sorry, but I must go before I wilt, my beautiful star. Please rest. Archie will need you when he's ready to talk. This news is jarring, especially for him." She gave Lyra a quick hug before leaving the pod.

Left to her own thoughts, Lyra picked up a piece of toast and spread a greenish-orange goo on it. The first bite was tangy, making her mouth water for more. After clearing her plate and finishing her tonic, she was still left feeling hungry.

With no one around, she used her skills for more. She thought, if she could move boulders with her mind, putting spread on a piece of toast wouldn't be too much of a challenge.

Lyra had the toast floating over her plate with ease and immediately understood the real challenge. A boulder was huge and heavy, but it was just one piece of material that her mind had to focus on. This little experiment would require manipulating many things at the same time.

The butter knife smoothly moved towards the bowl of goo, gracefully scooping a generous amount before gliding towards the toast. A proud smile spread across Lyra's face. Although it was not as smooth as she had wished, only a few drops ended up on the table.

Spreading the goo on to the toast proved to be more frustrating than it was worth. She snatched the knife in her hand and finished without using her skills. She angrily took a bite of her toast, causing the crumbs to scatter across the table.

Helix clapped, startling Lyra. She spun around and saw him smiling. There was someone unfamiliar next to him. She had shoulder length black hair with streaks of purple, almond-shaped brown eyes, and a fair complexion. She was slender, yet athletic. Lyra couldn't quite guess her age.

"Well done. Something so intricate and lightweight takes a great deal of patience and mind control," Helix said.

"Thank you," Lyra replied, not knowing what else to say.

"Lyra, meet Dara. Dara, this is Lyra," Helix said.

"Nice to meet you," Lyra said.

Dara nodded, not saying anything.

"Dara is here to help us figure out how Janus was able to do what he did," Helix said.

"Will it hurt?" Lyra asked.

Dara's hands made a few signals before Helix nodded.

"No pain. It will use a lot of your energy. Nebula will monitor your vitals. Dara would like to start now," Helix said.

"Nebula left to revitalize. I don't know how long that takes," Lyra said.

Dara made more signals with her hands.

"Dara said she can start without her and will send for her when needed. Are you ready?" Helix asked.

"I guess so," Lyra said, even though she wasn't sure. She took a few sips of water before standing to follow them into the hallway.

"Breathe. You're flickering," Helix said.

The walls were smooth, curved and very cave-like. Brightly lit torches along the path made them glow with a shimmery radiance. The torches were like magic, coming to life as they walked and dimmed behind them. Lyra wondered if Helix or Dara were making it happen or if the torches themselves could sense their presence. There was still much to learn about being a Walker.

They made several left and right turns before coming to a stop in front of a pod. Dara entered as Helix paused for Lyra to pass by.

This pod was smaller compared to the others she had seen in the Grotto.

Dara gestured for Lyra to get into the reclining chair, then took a seat next to it on a stool. The chair was covered in soft fabrics and natural colors that matched her training suit. There was a tall lamp in the corner, casting a warm glow and gentle heat, just like the ones in the kitchen.

Leaning back, Lyra experienced a sense of discomfort and anticipation of what was to come.

Dara gestured towards a stone table, where a bowl of tempting sweets awaited her. Lyra took one and popped it in her mouth. "Thank you."

As soon as the outer shell dissolved, she felt a chilling sensation that cooled her body internally. "Wow! How is that possible?" Lyra's eyes widened in surprise.

"They're called ice pops. They have an instant cooling effect." Helix laughed.

"A little different from what I call an ice pop." Lyra popped another one in her mouth, waiting for the burst of coolness.

Dara smiled, then gracefully moved her hands in a series of gestures.

Ever since Lyra became a Walker, she had understood a greater number of languages. She wondered why she couldn't understand what Dara was signing.

"Dara said to relax. She needs you to close your eyes and clear your mind," Helix translated.

"What is she…" Lyra stopped herself, realizing she was about to ask Helix when Dara was standing right there. "What are you going to do?"

Helix didn't wait for Dara to sign, "She's skilled in what Earth people call neuroscience or the function of the nervous system and the brain. She might learn how Janus interrupted your bend, sending you to another planet. You will feel a surge of energy that will raise your body temperature. When you heat up, eat an ice pop. You can have as many as you need," he said as he placed the bowl in her lap.

Lyra nodded, then leaned back again and closed her eyes.

"The ever-expanding universe accommodates many life forms. The ogres and elpinitida are not the scariest nor the most dangerous. There are far more lethal creatures out there. There's plenty of kindhearted and cuddly creatures, too. The universe thrives on a balance of good and bad. When someone tips the scale, the universe responds," Helix rambled.

"What are you talking about?" Lyra asked.

"Dara said to distract you. You're flickering again."

"Helix, that was so random." Lyra laughed.

"It worked. You're not flickering. You relax while I ramble," Helix said.

Taking a deep breath, Lyra closed her eyes and gripped the bowl of ice pops.

Helix continued, "Saros is tipping the scales, and the universe is struggling to keep that balance. She's gained a lot of followers and trained them well. Nebula has been one of her targets for years because she is a very valued healer. There are a few healers left. If Saros or her soldiers were to attack Alora, we need only to send lifelines to Walkers to help us defend Alora. We have an agreement with other planets to come to our aid as we would do for them. No one wants another battle like the one we had with Alectryon. We think that agreement has kept Saros away. However, we expect with her unnatural powers, by stealing from other Walkers, she will attack soon. She may not attack Alora directly, but she's already figured out a way to get you to another planet."

Lyra experienced a surge of intense heat, as if her body was burning from within. It was more uncomfortable than painful and caused her to sweat. She quickly popped an ice pop in her mouth, relieved when she felt the coolness.

"Dara says you're blocking her. Let your mental shields down for this to work. Focus on my words."

Lyra took a few deep breaths before dropping her shields again.

"Good. Now, where was I? Saros is destroying Walkers and stealing their skills. This has never been done. She's collecting rare skills to make herself more powerful than any Walker alive. Soon she will be unstoppable. There's a myth of a Walker who possessed more skills than any other. He was known as the Universe Walker. Legend has it he was born with his skills and yet, they ultimately cost him his life. He called on too many skills at once. The amount of energy it took to stay in control became unstable, breaking him into millions of particles. He literally burst, releasing his energy back into the cosmos. What makes Saros so dangerous? She will do anything to become the most powerful Walker. She has no boundaries. She kills others to gain more power. So, what kind of damage will she do before she bursts? Or maybe she's already figured out a way to prevent that. If so, the entire universe is in terrible danger."

The next blast of heat left Lyra with an instant migraine. She went to grab her head when she felt Helix hold her wrists, gently pushing them down towards her sides.

"It's almost over," Helix promised right before she went into the nothingness.

<h2 style="text-align:center">~Chapter 21~</h2>

Something cool touched her lips. "Lyra, it's an ice pop. You need to eat it," Helix insisted. His words were rushed as if concerned.

She welcomed the familiar coolness as it brought down her body temperature. Her clothes felt sticky and her body ached. "Is it over?"

"Yes. Don't get up," Helix demanded.

Lyra slowly opened her eyes, squinting against the dim light.

Helix held onto Dara, making sure she wouldn't fall to the floor. Her eyes half-closed and her body slouched forward.

"Nebula will be here soon with a few tonics. You'll both feel better once you drink them and sleep for a while." Helix handed her a cool rag with his free arm. "Put this on your head. It will help keep you cool and lessen the headache."

"Did Dara find anything?" Lyra asked.

"Yes. You're lacking an element called selenium. Without it, all the elements in your brain are thrown off balance. Janus confused your brain to change where you were bending. Thankfully, he can't actually control minds. It means he's been hiding that he is telepathic. That's how he's able to confuse your mind. He sends images instead of words, making your mind think that's where you want to bend. Now we know why Saros needs him," Helix said.

"Why didn't Saros destroy him and take the skill for herself? And how did we lose the selenium to begin with?" Lyra asked.

"To answer your first question, Saros might need others to do some of the dirty work for her. She can't do everything alone. I don't have an answer for the second question. We have the same concerns and will look into it."

"Now that Dara knows what to look for, will it be easier to check Archie?"

"Yes, and no. Dara needs to rest before trying something like that again and I need to update Galena as soon as Nebula gets here. Galena will need to be checked as well. Janus has had plenty of access to her over the years. We will figure this out," Helix said with a forced smile.

Nebula arrived only moments later with a cart full of tonics. Lyra laughed, knowing that she and Dara would have to drink them all before being released.

Nebula took two crimson tonics from the cart once she settled in and handed one to Lyra. Then she softly awakened Dara, pressing the other tonic into her hand. Helix said his goodbyes and left.

"Archie is on his way. After Dara confirms he lacks the same element, it's training time," Nebula said.

"Training already? Helix said Dara needs to rest first." Lyra said. The tonic was pleasantly tangy.

"We cannot waste time. Without selenium, you guys are in even more danger. It is an unstable element, so you and Archie need to learn how to conserve oxygen while floating in space. You guys are coming with us to collect it, then immediately inject it."

"How are we getting there if we can't bend?" Lyra asked.

"We're taking the stargazer," Nebula smiled.

Just as Lyra was going to ask about the stargazer, Archie and Pollux showed up.

"Did you miss me?" Pollux said.

Lyra avoided making eye contact with Archie. Instead, she stared at Dara, who had just emptied her tonic, and gave the boys a slight smile.

"Dara, you already know Pollux," Nebula said. "This is Archie. Archie, meet Dara."

"Hi." Archie waved, then said directly to Lyra. "I'm sorry."

Lyra was surprised and immediately turned her focus to him. "You have nothing to be sorry about. I'm sorry for the, um, the news," Lyra said, wishing she had a bracelet to fidget with.

Archie laughed. "I shouldn't be surprised by anything anymore. I mean, we're on another planet and we have skills that are like magic or superpowers. Anything is possible."

"I can't believe you're okay with this." Lyra scrunched her eyebrows in confusion.

"I'm not okay with it. I don't know what to think or how to feel. Honestly, I am numb. But I know that I'm not mad at you. I'm mad at her. We need to get your family back and my dad. I have a lot of questions for him." Archie moved closer. "It's my turn in the hot seat, I think."

Lyra got up, making room for Archie to sit. "It's all yours. You think your dad knew?"

"I don't know." Archie looked towards Dara. "Let's get this over with."

Dara made a few signs with her hands, her fingers gracefully dancing through the air. Nebula translated, "Dara said it will only take a few minutes because she now knows what she's looking for."

Lyra mouthed, *"Lucky"* before handing Archie a bowl. "When you heat up, eat one of these. They'll keep your temperature down."

Archie looked between Dara and Nebula before taking the bowl. He leaned back and closed his eyes.

Several minutes passed and half of the bowl of ice pops was gone when Dara gently released her hands from his temples. She signed her findings to Nebula. Nebula thanked her, then gave her another tonic. This time it was a silver-colored liquid.

"Archie also needs selenium. We'll leave in a few hours. I need to talk with Galena first, then prep the stargazer," Nebula said.

"What's a stargazer? Shouldn't Dara check Galena first?" Lyra asked.

"Dara is too exhausted. Galena and I will also be injected with selenium as a precaution. It won't hurt us either way. Since it's not safe to bend and we need to travel far, the stargazer will do the bending for us. Earth people would call it a spaceship, but it's very different. You'll see. Right now, I need you to go back to your pods and sleep.

You'll need your energy," Nebula said. "Pollux, can you walk them back, then show Dara to her pod?"

"Sure thing," Pollux replied. He helped Dara to her feet and supported her as they walked.

"Are you sure you're okay?" Lyra asked Archie while they walked the halls.

"No, but I will be. It's just a lot to process," Archie admitted.

"Yeah, it is," she agreed.

It was a short walk back to the pods. Lyra walked into her pod, waving to Archie as he went into his across the hall from her. The metal wall closed behind her and exhaustion hit her like a ton of bricks. The moment her head hit the pillow; she was fast asleep.

~Chapter 22~

Lyra woke a few hours later to Castor's voice. "Time to wake up. We need to be at the stargazer soon. Lyra, wake up."

Rubbing the sleep from her eyes, Lyra stretched her tired limbs. The nap wasn't long enough, and she still felt groggy. "To learn how to reserve oxygen, right?" Lyra grumbled.

"Yes. You have time for a quick shower. There's a change of clothes in the wash pod already. Meet me in the hall as soon as you're done."

Castor was gone before she could complain.

Lyra dragged herself out of bed and stumbled into the wash pod, still half-asleep. After a refreshing shower and a change of clothes, she felt more awake. She was excited to see the stargazer.

Pollux, Archie, and Castor were waiting just outside of Archie's pod.

"Took you long enough," Pollux teased.

"Easy for you to say. Dara didn't drain your energy," Lyra snapped.

"Easy now. I'm just playing," Pollux said. He put on his backpack and walked down the hall. "Let's go."

Castor wore an identical backpack. He jogged to catch up with Pollux, waving for Archie and Lyra to follow. After a few minutes, they stepped outside the Grotto. A warm breeze brushed against her face.

"Where are we going?" Archie asked.

"To the launch bays. We don't keep the stargazer in the Grotto. Since we can't bend, we have to walk. Oh, I almost forgot." He stopped to grab something out of his backpack. He pulled out four small pouches, handing two to Lyra and two to Archie. "One is water, and the other is soup. You bite, then sip on that part, like a straw."

"Cool design. Thanks," Archie said, then he took a sip. "How many stargazers are here?"

Everyone continued to walk. "We have one stargazer. They are few and far between these days. They were helpful during the war with Alectryon when wounded Walkers needed to be brought to safety for healing," Castor said.

They walked through the main village where people were going about their day. Some were bargaining prices for food and items, while others eagerly examined the merchandise.

Not too long after they passed through the village, fields with Alorans tending to their crops and mounds of boulders that were supposedly homes, they reached the outskirts. Lyra felt the air chill as they walked between towering boulders and into a tunnel.

"We're almost there." Castor announced, his words echoing off the walls.

Lyra strained her eyes as they adjusted to the dimly lit tunnel. Just like in the halls of the Grotto, torches magically came to life as they walked further in.

Approaching the entrance, the doors parted, and they were greeted by a set of guards granting them passage. They entered a pod with multiple hallways branching off in various directions, like a labyrinth.

"Galena and Nebula are waiting in bay one," a guard said.

"Thank you," Castor and Pollux said at the same time.

They walked down a short hallway that opened to the largest pod Lyra had ever seen. She stopped in the entrance, taking in the sight of what she assumed with the stargazer.

Nebula and Galena were standing in front of it. The twins and Archie joined her, but Lyra stayed back. The stargazer differed from what she'd imagined. It didn't have the shiny, futuristic appearance of a chrome alien craft, like in movies and cartoons. There wasn't a green glow coming from it and it wasn't shaped like a disk with beaming lights to suck up humans.

This spaceship, a stargazer, had an oblong shape and was a mixture of dark gray with some greens and reddish browns. Lyra walked closer, noticing a hint of silver where the light touched it.

"It's nothing like I imagined. It looks like an asteroid," Lyra whispered to Archie.

"Nothing," Archie replied. She noticed then that he was also mesmerized by it.

Lyra walked past Galena and Nebula, giving them a silent nod of greeting. There was a magnetic force pulling her towards the stargazer. She reached out, dragging her hand along its cool surface, feeling the grooves beneath her fingertips. She was surprised by its smoothness. There was a faint smell of hard-boiled eggs that made her crinkle her nose. Archie was only a few steps behind her, reaching out towards the stargazer.

"Wow," Archie gasped. His eyes were wide with wonder. "Do you *feel* that?"

"It feels like it's alive and smells like sulfur," Lyra said as she continued to skim her palm along the stargazer.

Archie laughed, waving a hand in front of his nose. "It does."

"You're feeling its energy," Galena said.

"It is very much alive." Nebula smiled. "This stargazer was a gift to Master from me. After the war, I used it to travel from galaxy to galaxy for many cosmic years. It was my home away from home." She gently placed her palm near Lyra's, softly humming a bittersweet melody.

Lyra felt the stargazer vibrate in sync with the song. "That's incredible."

"It is the song of her people," Galena explained.

"Why does it sound sad?" Archie asked, setting the palm of his hand on the stargazer again. "The vibrations match the song."

"The same song is used no matter the emotion. When there's sadness, the harmony represents that feeling. When there's happiness, the harmony changes. The person singing the song controls the mood, even though the words remain the same," Nebula explained when she finished singing.

"What are the words? I don't understand the language," Archie asked.

Lyra brushed a tear away. She felt like an intruder overhearing something she shouldn't have heard. Nebula's voice floated through the air once again, as she stood near the stargazer. The song's meaning was meant for the stargazer, yet Lyra understood. Nebula was feeling anxious about this journey, and the stargazer empathized with her.

"Another time, sweet child. Today we bend in this magnificent stargazer." Nebula smiled, but Lyra knew it wasn't a genuine smile. There was a hidden sense of sadness and concern.

Nebula touched the stargazer with only her fingertips and it responded by lowering a ramp for them to board.

"How is the stargazer going to bend without putting us at risk?" Archie questioned.

"Come. I will explain." Galena made her way up the ramp.

Lyra slowly followed everyone onto the stargazer. Running her fingers along the walls, she continued to feel vibrations. This left her in complete awe more than anything else. What she thought was an inanimate object was truly alive. She wondered if it could feel physical pain or if its being-like characteristics were limited.

"Does this stargazer have a name?" Lyra asked Nebula.

The switchboard's blinking lights illuminated Nebula's face. "Her name is in a forgotten language from people on my home planet. I'm not sure how to translate it." Nebula admitted. She held her hands over the switchboard, barely touching the keys. It was obvious she was mentally recalling the purposes of each one.

"I haven't heard any different languages since being on Alora." Archie said before looking over Nebula's shoulder at the switchboard.

"Have you heard yourself speak?" Galena giggled. She gestured for Lyra and Archie to take a seat across from her.

"Heard myself?" Archie asked. He took in every detail before sitting down.

Nebula laughed. "I guess we should have mentioned this sooner. All Walkers have the linguistic intuition skill, which means you can speak and understand many languages. It's extremely important to communicate with all life forms to prevent misunderstandings. Some languages have been lost, like the language of my people. My home planet was destroyed. I am one of the last of my kind. Even I've forgotten much of my native language."

"So, I have been speaking different languages without realizing? That's wild. What else can we do? Are you going to hand us a wand now, too?" Archie joked.

"No one is getting a wand. Those are for top-level, highly skilled Walkers with clearance to use them. They are for emergency situations only," Galena said.

Lyra deliberately avoided making eye contact with Archie. She was trying to keep herself from laughing, but she was doing a very poor job. She cupped her hand over her mouth. The moment

Archie snorted, she couldn't contain herself and burst out laughing.

"Galena, on Earth, there's a fictional character from a book series that finds out he's a wizard and gets a magical wand," Nebula explained. She winked at Lyra and Archie. "It's very different from the wands Walkers receive."

"Wait! Wands are real?" Lyra squealed. "I thought you guys were playing a joke on us."

"I'm not sure what to believe anymore. I guess I shouldn't be shocked by anything. I mean, we're on a spaceship disguised as an asteroid. It's genius!" Archie said.

"A wand for a Walker," Galena explained, "is a small quantum computer capable of harnessing a small amount of gamma rays from nearby black holes, neutron stars, or from a supernova explosion. That energy is capable of mass destruction if not used with good intent. Therefore, wands can only be activated by a DNA signature from its owner. There are only three wands that we know of. Two of them are in galaxies on the furthest outskirts of the universe. It would take them a few days' travel to get to Alora."

"I'm afraid to ask who has the third wand," Lyra admitted.

"Saros' father, Alectryon." Nebula said, watching Archie closely.

"I'm fine. Knowing who she is made me understand who he was. I'm sorry for what they have done. We will stop her."

"You have no reason to be sorry, Archer. You cannot control anyone's chosen path, nor should you feel responsible for their actions. Your choices will determine who you choose to be." Galena placed a hand over his. "Saros chose her own path and she will pay for what she has done."

Archie nodded, then Galena released his hand and leaned back in her seat.

"She's right, Archer. Your family does not define who you are," Nebula agreed.

"And you will not try to be a hero and sacrifice yourself to pay for their consequences," Lyra emphasized, standing with her hands on her hips in front of him.

Archie laughed. "Alright. Enough mushy stuff. I have a serious question. Can Saros use the wand if she shares Alectryon's DNA?"

"The chances of her being able to use it are slim. She only shares about 50% of Alectryon's DNA. From what we know, it has to be an exact match. We don't know where the wand is and haven't heard that she has it," Castor said.

"Good," Archie said.

Lyra's attention turned to the switchboard. "Why does it feel so alive?"

"You're feeling its energy," Nebula said.

"Can Janus use that to redirect our bend?" Archie asked.

"No, he can't. Stargazers are controlled by a quantum computer. It cannot be tracked, traced, or trailed while bending. I use the switchboard to input our destination. So, unless Janus is physically here watching what I do, he will not be able to find us," Nebula answered.

"We shouldn't be gone for long. Nebula will bring us to a nebula to quickly collect the selenium. Stargazers are fast," Galena said.

"We will teach you how to store your oxygen when we get there. It's really easy," Pollux said.

"Ready to launch?" Galena asked Nebula.

"Not yet. Everyone needs to get their SpaceTec suits on. The temperature will plummet as soon as I get started," Nebula said.

Castor and Pollux opened a storage bin, then pulled out something that looked like a spacesuit.

"Quantum computers require freezing temperatures to function. The suit will help keep you warm," Pollux said, handing one to Lyra.

Nebula got to work pressing a button and flipping switches on the switchboard while Castor and Pollux finished getting on their suits, then buckled into their watcher positions. They sat on opposite sides of the stargazer, looking for potential threats.

Lyra finished pulling her hood over her face, which had a clear window, and then securely buckled into her seat, making sure everything was in place before giving a thumbs up.

"Can you tell us the stargazer's name even if we can't understand it?" Lyra asked.

Nebula made a string of clicking and whooping sounds. When she was done, Lyra smiled. "I thought you said it was a forgotten language?"

"Did you not just hear all the odd noises Nebula made?" Archie asked, rubbing one of his ears through his hood.

"She called the stargazer Freyja. It's a beautiful name," Lyra said.

"How did you do that?" Nebula asked.

"Do what?" Lyra shrugged her shoulders.

"How did you understand the name, then translate it?" Nebula asked, scrunching her eyebrows.

"Once you said it, I remember seeing it on the switchboard," Lyra confessed.

"That symbol?" Archie asked, pointing to the switchboard.

"I see a name. When Nebula said it, it clicked and I knew how to pronounce it," Lyra confessed.

"Her mind was designed to decode. It makes sense," Castor added.

"Yes, I suppose so. Her mind probably does that when she reads, too. Always decoding. It would explain why words float off the paper and get jumbled around. There's nothing to decode in Earth books," Galena giggled.

"Your mind is powerful, Lyra. I'm curious to learn what else it can do," Nebula said.

"Unfortunately, we don't have a lot of time. We should get started," Galena announced.

The temperature plummeted and a soft vibration rumbled all around as the stargazer came to life, even more so than it already had.

"Here we go," Nebula said, pressing more buttons.

The stargazer jolted forward, throwing Lyra deep in her seat. They were moving faster than she had ever imagined possible. It felt like only minutes before the stargazer slowed, then stopped.

"Are you star-struck?" Pollux laughed. When no one responded, he added, "Get it? Starstruck because we're surrounded by stars."

"Funny." Lyra got out once her breathing returned to normal. Nothing had prepared her for the kaleidoscopic swirl of colors and the organic energy that surged all around them.

"In case of an emergency, you need to know how to retain your oxygen. Let's get started," Castor said to Lyra and Archie.

~Chapter 23~

Castor taught Lyra and Archie how to retain oxygen. It was something they instinctively did during a bend, so recognizing how to do it on command took less than three attempts.

"It's like we're looking at the universe's rainbow, but better," Archie said as he looked out the window.

Lyra agreed that being so close to the nebula made the colors brighter than any photo she'd seen. She couldn't figure out which nebula they were near though. "Which nebula is this?" Lyra asked.

"Not one within the Milky Way Galaxy, if that's what you're wondering." Nebula pressed a few buttons on the switchboard before speaking again. "Listen carefully. Gathering certain elements can be challenging, like selenium. It's unpredictable. The twins will assist me while you guys stay with Galena on the stargazer. As soon as I get back, I have to quickly prepare it to be injected."

"Why did we have to learn how to retain oxygen if we aren't going to help?" Lyra asked.

"No Walker should be out here without knowing how to retain oxygen. It's something you would've been taught if we had time to train you properly. It's good to know in case of an emergency," Castor said.

"Take your seats. We need to get closer." Nebula waited for everyone to buckle into their seats before she launched the stargazer closer to the nebula. They were surrounded by colorful gas and dust.

Lyra was so captivated by the nebula that she didn't realize Nebula and the twins had already left. She only realized she had been literally staring off into space when Galena called her name and told her and Archie to stand closer to the window. Then Galena pressed a few buttons on the switchboard. The stargazer's walls practically vanished, creating a massive window, leaving only the floor and ceiling untouched. They were immediately surrounded by a thick, luminous fog. Lyra closed her eyes, shielding them from the overpowering brightness.

"Oops. I forgot about that. There, that's better," Galena said.

When Lyra opened her eyes again, she saw that a polarized layer covered the windows, dimming the bright light.

"The elements are scattered all around us. The light comes from the radiation energized by newborn stars. It's incredible, isn't it?" Galena said.

"I can see why it's such a challenge to collect the elements when they are spread out. I bet it's boiling hot. I can feel it getting warmer in here. Is that a problem for the stargazer?" Archie asked.

Galena pressed a series of buttons and the temperature quickly dropped. "Thanks for the reminder."

To pass the time, Lyra and Archie asked questions about the stargazer and collecting elements. It wasn't long before the twins and Nebula returned with the selenium.

Nebula returned the windows to their normal size, then added a layer over them to completely block out any light. "This process is light sensitive. Give your eyes time to adjust to the dark. Stay in your seats while I prepare this. The sooner we get out of the open space and back to Alora, the better." Nebula quickly got to work in a small space set up as a mini lab.

"Don't bend until we get back to Alora in case it doesn't work," Galena added.

"And if it doesn't?" Archie asked, beating Lyra to the question.

"Then we will think of something else," Galena said.

As the moments passed, Lyra's eyes adjusted to the darkness. She could make out Archie's face since he was closest to her. With a gentle touch, Archie placed his hand on her knee, letting her know they would be okay. She hadn't realized she was bouncing her leg until then. She smiled at him, feeling calmer. Ever since she was little, she hated getting shots.

"Archie, you'll go first." Nebula held a rather intimidating looking needle before them. "Sit back and remove the suit from the top part of your arm. You'll feel a burning sensation as the selenium enters your muscles. It shouldn't be painful and I will be as quick as I can."

Archie looked pale, but he did what Nebula told him to do. Then he shut his eyes and tilted his head back. Lyra stood beside him, tapping her fingers on his other arm to distract him. She learned it from her mom when her little sister got hurt and they needed Nova to stay calm while her mom took care of the wound.

Nebula quickly poked Archie's arm with the needle, causing him to flinch. Moments later, Nebula was done. She put a Band-Aid with a floral print on his arm. "Doing alright?"

"That really hurt," Archie admitted, then as if realizing what he said, "But not too bad. You'll be fine." He forced a half smile. "Flowers? Seriously?"

"It's all we had," Nebula said. Then turned to Lyra. "Sit, my beautiful star. Let's get this over with."

"You're flickering, Lyra. Calm your breathing. If that attracts Janus, we're going to be like sitting bait out here. Please, sit. It will be over quickly." Galena said.

Lyra took a deep breath and sat down, leaning her head back like Archie had. Without thinking, she threw up a shield around her mind the second before Nebula injected the needle into her arm.

"All done," Nebula said. "Archer, do you feel any different?"

Whaam! Klank!

Boosh!

"What was that?" Archie yelled.

The stargazer jolted forward, throwing them all off balance.

"Something hit Freyja's left side!" Lyra yelled. A strange pain shot down her legs. "Why does my left side hurt?"

"We share Freyja's energy, so you can sense any damage to her," Nebula said. She pressed buttons on the switchboard, which opened the windows, giving everyone a better view of what was around them.

They had been pushed further away from the nebula. It wasn't as bright, which gave them the advantage of seeing anything approach them. Lyra stared outside, looking for any movement.

"Nothing should be out here. I checked the weather. There weren't any meteor showers on the radar," Castor said, looking out the window. Lyra noticed him preparing the weapons.

Whaam! Klank!

Boosh!

"That's not a meteor shower. Everyone to their seats and buckle," Galena said.

The stargazer was tossed from side to side. Flames erupted in front of the window, casting a brilliant orange glow that faded within seconds. If the stargazer's quantum computer got too hot, it would disable its ability to bend them to safety. Lyra's heart raced as she clicked her last buckle in place.

"We need to get out of here," Galena ordered.

Nebula was fast to work, pressing buttons in a panic. The stargazer jumped forward, but not far enough away.

"We can't bend. They've paralyzed us." Nebula's hands hovered over the switchboard, unsure of what to do.

"You said we couldn't be tracked," Archie snapped.

"We can't be tracked," Nebula hissed. She spun them around to face the direction they'd been hit.

"It could be a Walker with the skill of psionic energy," Castor yelled from the back corner. His face was close to the window and his hand was ready to pull the trigger. "I don't see anyone. Lux?"

"Nothing," Pollux replied.

"The skill of psionic energy, using mind energy to manipulate technology, right?" Archie asked.

At that moment, Lyra realized what had happened. In the seconds it took to protect her mind from feeling the pain of the needle, it must have opened her mind enough for Janus to find them. Janus was behind this. She was sure of it. She opened her mouth to tell them, then shut it. She couldn't get the words out to tell anyone.

Nebula nodded. "Even if someone had that skill, it would be a matter of pure luck to track us. Quantum computers use unpredictable qubits. They don't have the same transistors. They're impossible to track."

"That also means we can change where we're going during a bend to mask the evidence and throw them off course. It will buy us time to figure out how they tracked us," Archie suggested.

"How do you know all of that?" Galena asked.

"My dad's team at work is working on creating the first reliable quantum computer on Earth. It's all he talks about." He shrugged his shoulders.

"No one tracked us," Lyra forced out. "I did this. I opened my mind for a second, almost like bending before I closed it off to protect it from feeling the pain of the needle. Janus must have been waiting. I'm so sorry."

Whaam! Klank!

"They're attaching to the stargazer. This is not good," Pollux said.

"They're attached on my side too. We can't bend. It could set them off," Castor said.

"My beautiful star, you are not to blame. There's another way. Archer and Lyra, do you think you can bend back to Alora?" Nebula asked.

"I can't tell," Archie said.

"Me either," Lyra agreed.

"Can Janus bend inside the stargazer and attack us?" Archie asked.

"No. We have a protector aboard and they know it." Nebula ground her teeth.

"Who?" Lyra yelled over the sound of another blast.

"Me," Nebula said, "I can use my mental energy to make a temporary shield around us and give everyone enough time to bend out of here. The twins and Galena will bend with you to Earth, since it's too far to bend straight to Alora. From there, you can bend to Alora when you get some energy back. Walkers have limits. Earth is only a galaxy away. Saros is not just after you guys." Nebula was shaking.

"Why?" Archie asked.

"I have a rare skill that she wants," Nebula said.

Whaam! Boosh!

An alarm sounded. Archie unbuckled and stood in front of the switchboard next to Nebula. He carefully watched as she worked to turn the alarm off. Lyra noticed the twins were having a silent conversation while Galena was frozen where she sat. They were in trouble, and it was all her fault. She had to find a way to get them out of this.

"Everyone needs to bend to Earth now," Nebula demanded, holding onto her chair so hard that her knuckles turned white.

"No! No sacrifices. We are not losing you. There has to be another way," Lyra yelled.

"We will not lose you," Galena said. She walked closer to Nebula and placed her hand on Nebula's shoulder. "We'll figure this out together."

"It's the only choice we have," Nebula said, tears flowing down her face. "Let me do this for you, for them."

"We have another option," Archie said. Then, without asking, he pressed a few buttons. "I need at least three and a half minutes. Outer space is a negative 454.81 degrees Fahrenheit. That's a few degrees colder than what a quantum computer needs to operate. I think I can cool down the stargazer and shake those things off. If we're quick enough, we can bend before they reattach."

"Archer, you're brilliant!" Nebula smiled. "That could work. Cas and Lux, can you buy us time?"

"We can bend out there and create a distraction," Pollux suggested. Castor was wide eyed in shock at the suggestion.

"That's too dangerous," Galena objected.

"We'll create a distraction from opposite sides and be back before they can attack us. We're already in danger," Pollux said.

"Unfortunately, he's right. This could work," Castor agreed.

Galena nodded, "I hope the universe is on our side. Be safe. Be quick."

The twins vanished.

Prying the freezer open, Archie turned towards Lyra with a mischievous grin. She was familiar enough with him to recognize that look as a sign of a carefully thought-out decision. Just like him, she had complete confidence in his plan.

As the temperature dropped, Lyra sensed another energy. Since Janus knew where they were and she'd had the selenium injection, she took a chance and sent out a wave of mental energy. She didn't think there would be any more consequences, being that they were already in danger.

Her mind immediately collided with a familiar energy. She screamed.

"Easy now," Janus said into her mind.

Lyra gripped her chair and shut her eyes to concentrate on the energy. She could feel her heart pounding in her chest as she desperately thought of something to say. This could be the distraction Archie needed. This could keep Janus focused on her and not the twins. This was how she'd make it right. She just had to get him to talk, which wouldn't be hard to do.

"So, you can neurobond. Have you figured out the fun part?" Janus asked.

"And you can, too. It was smart of you to hide that skill from Galena," Lyra said.

"Do you know the best part of this skill? Open your eyes to see for yourself."

Lyra slowly opened her eyes, the image coming into focus. She wasn't on Frejya, but on another stargazer with some of Saros' soldiers. In a panic, she shut her eyes again and screamed.

"Stop screaming. You are not actually on my stargazer. You are simply seeing through my eyes as I am through yours. That's all I needed to verify. How did you get Nebula to leave Alora?"

Lyra felt foolish. *"How?"*

"It's part of the skill." He laughed.

"What do you want?" She needed to keep him talking.

"You know WHO I want. Don't worry. I'll be back for you and Archer soon enough."

"You can't have her," Lyra said.

"If Archer thinks throwing the weights off will work, he'll be very disappointed to learn that he needs a code to deactivate them. Separating them without the code will detonate them. Warn him now," Janus demanded.

"You're lying," Lyra said.

"Have it your way. Once Archie activates the bombs, Nebula will be forced to shield everyone. While you run away, she'll be mine for the taking. All I have to do is wait," Janus said.

"You're the one who ran away after attacking your own sister."

"I didn't attack her. Ask her what really happened. Archer can tell if she's lying or not. You're on the wrong side, Lyra."

"Whatever, Janus. Once a liar…"

"Always a liar. Like my sister. Like my father. She's the one who's lying. You're running out of time. Warn them before you become cosmic bits and pieces," Janus said before breaking the connection.

Lyra felt her body shaking.

"Lyra. Lyra!" Nebula yelled.

"Janus," Lyra blurted out, "he knows you're on the ship. He saw," she said, gasping for air. "He saw you through my eyes. He can neurobond. Archie, listen to me. He said you will set them off if you try to separate them without a code. I think he's telling the truth. He wants Nebula to shield us so we can get away then he plans on taking her."

"Yes, I know. We have less than a second to bend or we're all dead. We need to do this now," Archie urged.

"You know?" Lyra questioned.

"Yes. Hold hands. It's time," Archie said.

"We're ready," Galena said, reaching her hand out towards Lyra.

The twins were back, holding hands and waiting. Once Lyra grabbed hold of Galena, Archie joined them.

"Now," Archie yelled.

Lyra felt the bitter cold nip at her, tearing her particles apart, but this time she saw colors. Beautiful colors swirling all around her. She focused on one of them, pushing her energy into it.

~Chapter 24~

Lyra smelled fresh herbs and knew she was in the healing pod. Gradually, she opened her eyes and squinted to shield herself from the lights. The brightness was overwhelming, so she closed her eyes tightly.

She couldn't remember what happened.

Like she'd done before, she stretched her mind out to check for injuries. She felt skin pulling and puckering, as if it had been stretched too tight.

Stitches.

To stop herself from panicking, she took slow, deep breaths. When she felt calmer, she continued to scan her body and found that her arm, side, and left leg all had stitches. There was an IV in her other arm and bandages wrapped in different places of her body. She felt a dull burning sensation under the wraps. Had she been burned? Why were there so many stitches? She had so many questions.

She couldn't concentrate over the loud humming and whooshing noises that seemed to surround her. It almost sounded like she was inside a vacuum.

She tried opening her eyes again, but found it to be too bright and painful.

Wiggling her fingers, Lyra was happy to find that she could move them. She extended her arm until it came in contact with something cold and hard.

"I wouldn't move if I were you," a strange voice warned her.

"*Who are you?*" Lyra said into the strange mind.

"*Nobody. Galena, I guess, um, summoned me or whatnot. They didn't have another way to communicate with you. Lucky me,*" he responded dryly.

An orange hue danced in her mind when he spoke. She wondered if it had something to do with her injuries. Maybe she hit her head too hard.

"*I'm not in the healing pod, am I?*" Lyra asked.

"*We're on a wonderfully polluted planet called Earth. The air is awful and the food is even worse.*"

Ignoring his comments, she asked, "*Where's Archie?*"

"*Your boyfriend is fine. He couldn't get through to you, so they dragged me here.*"

"*He's my best friend, not my boyfriend. Did I do or say something for you to not like me?*"

"*It's nothing personal. I assumed he was your boyfriend. He sure acts like it.*"

Lyra thought about that. If Archie was that upset, it could only mean one thing. "*Can you tell me if anyone else was hurt?*" Lyra asked.

"*You were…severely. I'm amazed we can talk right now.*"

"*Anyone else?*"

"*Nothing serious. From what I heard Nebula threw an energy shield around everyone before you could injure them.*"

"*Me? Injured them? Tell me what happened, please?*" Lyra begged.

"*Nebula will want to know that you can't remember.*" She heard him sigh before he continued. "*Apparently, you have many skills, including pyrokinesis.*

Archie detached the bombs then you threw them at the other stargazer. Nebula immediately got everyone out of there, but somehow, a bomb reattached before the bend. One bomb put a hole in the stargazer, blasting flames inside. They said you burst into flames, trying to direct the fire outside, but pieces of the stargazer shot like bullets everywhere. You were badly cut and lost concentration. Nebula threw out a shield, but she couldn't protect you while you were on fire. She said she saw you fight the chemical fire with natural fire. The chemical fire burned you before you could direct away. Blue said you are fireproof to natural fire and he thinks you are truly remarkable. He can't stop saying it. I just love hearing it every single second of every single day on this blasted planet."

"I don't remember any of that."

"The stargazer was destroyed and Alora was too far away. Archie apported everyone to Earth. Blue thinks he's great too. What do you want me to tell them?" he asked.

"Please tell them I'm fine and would like to know when I can open my eyes."

"You're not fine, Lyra. You can't see what I see. Be thankful for that."

"Show me."

"I was given strict orders to not do that. They blindfolded me."

"Fine. When can I move again?" she asked, irritated because he knew much about her and she knew nothing about him.

"I don't know for sure. Maybe a week, maybe longer. Nebula said bending would cause more damage.

Ever travel by a hypervelocity star? They can travel trillions of miles per hour. It's an idea, but the weather isn't calling for any and they can be tricky to catch."

"Funny," Lyra said with a hint of sarcasm. If she had to deal with him for another week, she would at least try to get to know him better. *"Where are you from?"*

"Don't want to know my name first?"

"Sure. What's your name?"

"My name is Thamos. Friends call me Tom. You can call me Thamos."

"Nice to meet you, Thamos. I can't waste another week. It's all I ever seem to do these days. Get hurt…heal…get hurt…heal. I need to get out of here and find my family."

"Then do something about it. You have more skills than most Walkers. I've heard all the theories, but what if Saros gave you and Archie some of her stolen skills and that's why you guys have so many? It makes sense, right?"

Lyra was shocked by his questions. She hadn't had time to think that much about it. What if Saros had given her and Archie some of her stolen skills? It would explain why they had so many rare skills. It would explain why she wanted them. It wouldn't explain why she messed with Lyra's bracelet and tried to hurt her. Thamos was on to something, though.

"Did you tell anyone your theories?"

"Why? No one listens to me. I'm only here because Archie can't talk to you, and no one knows why. Oh, I

was supposed to let Nebula know when you woke and if I can talk with you. I'll be right back."

Lyra couldn't hear anything over the loud noises. She was left to her own thoughts. She wondered what other skills she had, if any. How would she know what they were? Could she self-heal? Then she remembered something strange.

In a video, one of her teachers made the class watch, it said something about cells needing oxygen to heal. It clicked, and she knew exactly why it sounded like a vacuum.

"Are you there?"

"Yup. I'm back. Nebula said to rest."

"I will, but first, what's the machine called that I'm in?"

"Nebula calls it a hyperbaric chamber. She said the polluted Earth air will cause an infection to your open wounds. She's not taking any chances."

"So, hyperbaric means?"

"You're being exposed to 100% oxygen with the pressure set to max. Nebula said doing this will speed up the healing process. She wants to bend you to Alora, as soon as possible."

"Are we in my house?"

"We're in some house Blue and Helix suggested."

"I know where we are."

"Nope, a different house. Saros' soldiers tore that one apart."

"How do you know so much?"

"It's the only thing anyone talks about. Plus, my father talks super loudly when he tells my mom about

his missions and thinks I'm fast asleep. He's not happy about me being here, but my mom insisted."

"Helix?"

"Wow. Is that another skill? I didn't expect you to get it right so fast."

"Not a skill. Something happened, and he's been trying to protect you since."

"Don't ask," Thamos said.

"I won't," Lyra said even though she wanted to ask about it. "Can you tell me what everyone is doing since I can't see yet?"

"I'm blindfolded and they're in another room. This machine takes up a lot of space."

"Can you let Nebula know that I'm going to use mental energy to boost the healing process?"

"I knew it. You can regenerate. Not surprised," he sighed.

"I don't know if I can. I want to try."

"I'm sure you can. There's nothing you can't do. It's like you and Archie are Galena's little prized possessions and no one else matters."

"They brought you here for a reason," Lyra retorted.

"I can only mentally communicate with you because you can neurobond. I can't do this with anyone else. Once you're healed, you should be able to communicate with everyone again. It takes a lot of mental energy, and Nebula thinks that's why Archie can't talk with you. Then I won't be needed. They'll send me home, far from my dad, where no one else can neurobond."

Lyra immediately understood why he didn't like her. He would be cast aside, unable to use his skill and unable to see his dad once she healed. *"I'm sorry."*

"Like I said, it's not personal."

"Will you let Nebula know what I'm about to do?"

"Yeah. Fine. Be right back."

With nothing else to do, she focused on her wounds. Unsure of how to go about healing herself, she started with sending a little burst of energy to the smallest one. Nothing happened.

"Nebula said to wait," Thamos's voice boomed in her mind. *"There's a Walker who can regenerate. Galena already sent for them."*

"That's good news. I don't think I could do it, anyway. Thanks, Thamos."

"It's Tom."

~Chapter 25~

Over the next few days, Lyra healed enough to move into a regular bed. She slept for most of the day and night. Nebula said sleeping was part of the healing process.

Even with the aid of a Walker whose name she didn't know, Lyra was still too weak to bend to Alora. The Walker used the regeneration skill to speed up Lyra's healing process. She drifted in and out of sleep, barely remembering anything. She had a vague recollection of arguing with Helix. He absorbed her pain, sparing her from feeling it, but it cost him his own health. She thought it was unfair for him to bear her pain. He dismissed her with a wave and refused to listen further.

After a few days of this, she finally woke, feeling more like herself. Nebula had a fresh bowl of fruit and hot soup waiting for her. Nebula complained that Earth people used way too many chemicals in their food, so she sent the twins back and forth to Alora for ingredients.

The Walker who had helped her heal left before Lyra could thank them. Shortly after that, Helix decided it was time to take Tom back to his mom on their home planet. Helix planned on staying with his family until he fully recovered.

Lyra and Archie played board games to pass the time and asked questions. They discovered the reason behind her loss of telepathic communication with Archie. Nebula explained that without the right amount of selenium, her mind and Archie's were weaker. That's how Janus could interfere with Lyra's bend. Their minds were healed by the selenium injection, but sadly, it hindered their ability to communicate telepathically.

Lyra was surprised when Nebula finally agreed to let her and Archie have food from their favorite place. They practically inhaled their protein-style hamburgers and salty fries from In-N-Out. Even the twins and Blue devoured their meals. Of course, Nebula encouraged everyone to drink various tonics to detoxify their bodies, but she winked when Lyra caught her stealing a fry from Blue when he wasn't looking.

"Good news," Blue announced. "You're going home today."

"To Alora?" Lyra asked.

"Yes. The twins went ahead to double check safety measures. Then they are tasked with training the people of Alora for a potential invasion. We have reason to believe Saros will attack soon," Blue said.

"The sooner we get you guys back to Alora, the sooner you can get back to training. You need to protect yourselves no matter what planet you're on," Nebula said.

"Helix is already back to work. He was supposed to gather as many Walkers as he could when he found Janus," Blue said.

"Is he okay? I mean, Helix. Is Helix okay?" Lyra asked.

"Helix is fine. He found Janus severely hurt. We have him in custody. Once we have you situated at the Grotto, Nebula and I will take care of Janus. He might tell us where your parents are being held if we offer to heal him," Blue said.

"Did he tell Helix anything?" Lyra asked.

"Helix thinks it could be a trap. It was too easy to find him and Janus was talkative. He thinks Archie destroyed his stargazer. And in his rambling, he gave hints of where Saros is, but nothing about your families. We should know more when we get back to Alora." Blue smiled. "You've healed nicely. The cuts are barely noticeable."

"Nebula is very talented," Lyra agreed.

"I was not able to heal the one on your shoulder to my liking. It will remain, but the rest will fade in time," Nebula said.

"Time to go," Blue said.

"I need to finish packing. Will you help me?" Nebula asked Blue. He nodded and they started getting the rest of her healing supplies together.

"I almost forgot." Archie reached into a hidden pocket of his training suit. He held out a bracelet to Lyra. "It's not exactly like the one your parents gave you, but here…it's…I made it for you."

Lyra held out her arm and Archie clasped the new bracelet on her wrist. She rotated his wrist around to get a better look at it. It looked so similar to the one her parents gave her. Instead of the Lyra constellation, the half-glass ball had the Milky Way galaxy with billions of the tiniest stars.

"It's beautiful, Archie. Thanks." Lyra sniffled back tears that threatened to escape.

"Did you know there aren't any real shooting stars? What Earth people see are—" Archie began.

"Are small meteors burning up as they enter the earth's atmosphere." Lyra finished his sentence.

"We will find them. I know we will." Archie got close enough to hug her and whispered, "We need to talk—alone." Then gave her the quickest hug before stepping back.

Lyra nodded.

"Oh, I almost forgot," Archie said. "Let me show you what it does."

"The bracelet does something?" Lyra asked.

"When you bend, you use a lot of mental energy, right? So, this is filled with quantum energy. It's not like mental energy and you can't use it the same way, but you can use it to boost your mental energy. Just open your mind to it and a photon will boost your energy. Cool, right?" Archie beamed.

"I don't know what a photon is or why it will help, but I'll use it wisely," Lyra laughed.

"You'll know what I mean when you try it. You should use one on the way back to the Grotto. Galena is waiting for us. See you in a few." Archie didn't wait for her response, shimmering into particles before he was completely out of sight.

"I need to get the healing pod ready for your arrival. Blue will bend back with you." Nebula slung a bag over her shoulder and shimmered away.

"Ready?" Blue asked.

"I think so." Lyra looked down at the bracelet, twirling it like she used to do with her old bracelet.

"He's tested it a bunch of times. It's safe." Blue extended his hand for her to take.

Lyra took his hand. "Ready." She opened her mind to the bracelet. A little light sparked in her mind, giving her a powerful boost of energy.

She faintly heard Blue scream. The bracelet doubled her speed of thought. Their particles were sent into a whirlwind of chaos. Lyra quickly threw out a protective shield around them. Then they materialized just outside the healing pod. Lyra laughed when Blue grabbed onto the nearest wall for balance.

"Archie! It worked!" Lyra said, looking around for Archie.

"He's not back. Neither is Nebula," Blue pointed out.

"They left before us," Lyra said.

"You shielded us. You're a protector," Blue laughed.

Nebula arrived, then Archie.

"How did you guys make it here before us?" Nebula asked.

"Archie can explain," Lyra said.

"Since no one is hurt, it will have to wait," Galena announced as she walked into the meeting pod. "Saros agreed to meet with me, but on one condition. She wants to meet here…tonight."

"Please, tell me you declined?" Blue stated.

"I agreed to give her clearance near the Froid only and for a limited time," Galena announced.

"You have time to get cleaned up, change, even rest before we will meet back here. I have a few things I need to do first. The twins will join us once they are done securing the area we agreed to let Saros land."

Blue rushed after Galena, who had already left and was probably halfway down the hallway. Lyra remained staring in the direction they had gone, wondering why she saw a green glow outlining Blue's body right before he left. This was the second time she noticed a color like that. She wondered if it could be a side effect of the selenium. She decided it could wait until her and Archie had time to talk with no one around.

Before they left to go to their pods, Archie said to Lyra, "I'm going to make as many photon bracelets as I can. Come help me when you're done, okay?"

Lyra was about to reply when she saw a faint greenish glow outlining Nebula's body. "You're green, just like Blue," she blurted out.

"What?" Nebula said.

"Nothing. Never mind. I think I need a nap." Lyra shook her head, hoping no one heard what she'd said.

No one moved, obviously waiting for her to explain. Archie crossed his arms and tapped his foot.

"What?" Lyra shrugged her shoulders.

"You see colors?" Nebula asked.

"You can't?" Lyra tried to make a joke but clearly no one was falling for it.

"You said Nebula *was* green, which she normally is, but you said she was green just like Blue. What does that mean?" Archie asked.

"I started seeing colors that outline people after the selenium injection. Nebula is a brighter and darker shade of green than Blue. I can still see it," Lyra confessed, feeling self-conscious for being the only who sees colors around people.

"My beautiful star, you're seeing auras," Nebula said. "It's like what Janus sees when he reads someone's potential. Each color means something, and the brightness or dullness gives away someone's intentions. It takes time and training to know what it all means. It can be a very useful skill."

Nebula extended her hand, conjuring a small spherical fruit-like object. She gestured for Lyra to take it. "It will dull the colors to make them less distracting for now. We need to focus on keeping you and Archer safe. Tomorrow we will find another Walker with the same skill to train you."

"How?" Lyra asked.

"One of my skills, remember? You can chew it, it's soft in the middle," Nebula said.

"Will this affect my other skills?" Lyra asked, holding the thing between her pointer and thumb.

"It only dulls the colors. It will not weaken your other skills. They're called colorcalmers. Without it, the colors will become more intense and can cause a headache and dizziness. Once you start training, you won't need them anymore. We need to be focused for tonight. I don't like this at all. I hope

Galena knows what she's doing. I have to go tend to Janus and find out whatever he's willing to give up."

"Can you two find your way to your pods?" Blue asked.

Lyra and Archie nodded.

"Good. I'm coming with you in case he tries something funny," Blue said to Nebula.

~Chapter 26~

Lyra quickly showered and changed into a clean training suit then rushed to Archie's pod. She saw him sitting on the floor, surrounded by beads and metal fragments. There were several small jars with brightly glowing objects. He was focused on making a bracelet when she cleared her throat.

When that didn't get his attention, Lyra walked closer. "Hi."

Without looking up, Archie said, "Something huge is happening tonight. I heard Galena and Helix arguing. Galena is trading herself for Nova and your mom. Saros won't agree to release my dad or yours. Nebula knows about it. Helix is against it. I don't know if Blue or the twins are in on it, but I think they are and I think everyone has a plan to make sure Galena doesn't go through with it."

Lyra didn't know what to say. Hearing what Galena was willing to do for her family was overwhelming. She sat on the floor near Archie, making sure not to disturb his work. She needed a few minutes to let the information sink in. Then she realized how bizarre the plan sounded. Galena would never leave her planet without a ruler. It would mean chaos for Alora.

"It doesn't make sense. Why would Galena do that? This is a trap. Saros isn't going to hand my sister and mom over that easily. She wants Nebula and you and me. No one has ever mentioned her wanting Galena. And Galena always puts her planet first. She wouldn't agree to give it all up."

"Helix asked the same thing. I was close enough to tell that Galena was telling the truth, though. I think there's more to it, too. I just don't know what. I don't understand why she wants your dad and my dad. I don't think she ever even loved my dad."

"None of this makes sense." Lyra sighed.

"I think we should tell them that we know and maybe they will include us."

"Or we can come up with our own plan?" Lyra suggested. She picked up a little metal piece and rolled it between her fingers. Archie had all the pieces sorted and labeled on trays. She mindlessly put the little metal piece back in its spot, then stood. "We can't let Galena sacrifice herself. I want to see my mom and sister so bad, but there has to be another way. I want my dad back too and I'm sure you want yours. I just don't know how…"

"I want to finish these bracelets because without them, we don't have a chance. Not against someone as powerful as Saros," Archie said, not looking at her as he worked.

Lyra noticed his hands slightly tremble as they hovered over the pieces. They hadn't talked about his mom since learning her true identity.

"If you want to talk about, um, your mom, I'm here for you."

"My *mom* died a long time ago. I have nothing to say about her," Archie snapped. "Sorry. I don't think of Saros as my mom. She means nothing to me and I want to keep it that way."

Lyra uncomfortably shifted from one foot to the other. "I understand." And she could. It would be easier to face Saros if Archie thought of her as anything other than the mother he cherished.

They didn't speak for a while. Lyra relaxed in a chair, watching Archie make bracelet after bracelet. She doodled on a blank piece of paper, trying to think of ways they could stop Saros without sacrificing Galena or anyone else.

"Galena is taking a long time to call us to that meeting," Archie said.

"Yeah. At least you're getting the bracelets done. Any ideas of how we can stop Saros yet?"

"Actually, yes." Archie held his hand out, showing her seven bracelets. "We'll say that we're delivering them to Nebula and the twins, which we will. I'll give the guards one for Galena, Helix and Blue before we leave. This one is mine. Oh, hand me yours so I can add more photons. And we'll need to dress warm." Archie flashed a mischievous grin. He was definitely up to something and by the way he was bouncing with energy, she knew he had something good planned.

"I'll be right back," Lyra said.

Her pod was right across the hall. She made her way inside, looking for a thicker suit meant for colder weather. She quickly grabbed it, then ran back to Archie's pod.

Struggling to catch her breath, Lyra asked, "Why don't you use your skill to send the bracelets to everyone?"

"I don't know where everyone is and we need an excuse to leave the Grotto."

"Makes sense. What's the plan?" Lyra asked

"I'll tell you on the way. We should leave before Galena calls us to that meeting." Each bracelet was carefully wrapped by Archie with a handwritten note, using soft cloth and string to secure them. Once he had his bracelet on his wrist, he held the other three packages, all neatly wrapped, and gave her three.

They walked past the guards stationed at the end of the hall without trouble, but the sound of footsteps behind them revealed they were being followed. Lyra wanted to ask if Archie had noticed, since they couldn't communicate telepathically anymore. She looked at him, arching her eyebrows in the direction of the guards. He nonchalantly shook his head, dismissing the issue, and continued on.

On their way to Galena's pod, Archie stopped in front of a few guards. He explained what were in the packages, then handed them over. He told them that he had to get the other bracelets to Nebula and the twins before the meeting and to let Galena know that they would be back soon.

They turned to leave and walked back down the hallway when Lyra noticed they were being followed again by a pair of guards. "What about..." she tilted her head towards the guards behind them.

"Don't worry. They can't bend." Archie grinned.

~Chapter 27~

Archie held his hand out and Lyra grabbed hold without hesitation. They ran outside, guards screaming after them to stop, but it was too late. Lyra cleared her mind, allowing Archie to bend them away from the Grotto.

They materialized near the border of the Froid. Lyra immediately felt a chill, like a thin sheet of ice had settled on her winter training suit. Her exposed face was met with a sharp, icy breeze that made her shiver. She wrapped her arms around herself as she looked around.

It was surprisingly loud, like she was in a wind tunnel. There wasn't much to see beyond the veil of nothingness. The Froid was completely dark with sudden bursts of lightning. She waited for another burst in hopes of it illuminating the area long enough for her see what it really looked like.

They were standing far enough away that Lyra didn't feel like they were in danger, but close enough to get caught in the high winds and freezing temperature.

There was a loud crack of lightning and a roar of thunder.

Archie tapped her shoulder. She turned and missed out on seeing any part of the Froid. He was yelling something but it was too loud and she couldn't hear what he was saying.

"I. Can't. Hear. You." Lyra yelled back.

Archie continued to yell, yet the words were lost in the wind.

Lyra shut her eyes, channeling her mental energy to communicate her thoughts to Archie, just as she had done previously. She gave them an extra boost by using a photon from her bracelet, then opened her eyes to see if it worked.

Archie staggered backwards. *"Not so loud,"* he yelled into her mind.

"It worked. It actually worked. You can hear me again?"

"I think you were trying to send your thoughts at the same time I opened my mind to you. Try again." Archie's words were clear in her mind again.

Lyra thought of something to say then sent her thoughts to him. He shook his head from side to side.

She gave it another try.

Nothing.

Archie motioned for her to continue by spinning his hand in a circle.

She thought of something funny. When he laughed, she wondered if he had been playing a joke on her. *"Did you hear me the entire time?"* Lyra asked.

"No, I had to find the right door to open in my mind. I don't think the injection took our telepathy away. I think it made our shielding stronger and closed our minds off, like locking a door. You have to find the right door to open. At least that's how it works for me. Try it."

It took Lyra a few tries until she found the right door to open and close. She opened and closed her mind to him, memorizing the feeling. She wondered if everyone had a different door. It's possible that she had her door open when Tom spoke to her, but Archie's door was closed, explaining why he couldn't communicate with her when Tom could. With time running out, she knew she would have to push that thought to the side for later.

"Ok. Now that I can hear you. Why are we here?" Lyra asked.

"I think Saros is using this meeting to capture us and I sense Galena is lying. Why would Saros give up your mom and sister, but not your dad or my dad? Why would Galena give herself up? Everyone seems to have their own plan and none of them include us. So, we are making our own plan."

Lyra had the same questions. Even so, she learned to trust Galena and the others. *"Rulers have secrets, Galena is no different."*

Archie cut her off. *"This feels different."*

"What if she is lying to keep us safe?"

"Possibly. It's just that none of this makes sense."

"I'm scared I won't get my family back or your dad. I want to trust that Galena has a good plan," Lyra cried.

"I'm scared too," his voice whispered in her mind.

Just then, a deafening boom reverberated through the air. It wasn't like the thunder she heard earlier.

Another boom. Louder. Closer. Dust and small pebbles were picked up as the air swirled around them.

"You're invisible. We're safe here."

"No, we're not. We have to get out of here. We should go to the meeting and hear what Galena has to say anyway."

"Yeah. Maybe I can figure out what Galena is hiding." Archie held his hand out for her to take.

They both froze when a loud female voice cut through the wind. "You're brave to have come alone."

Saros.

Lyra watched in horror as an overwhelming arrival of stargazers descended from the sky. They were trapped between the Froid and the stargazers. She wondered if this was a part of Saros' plan. In search of Saros, she looked for a stargazer with a downward ramp. She wondered how it was possible to hear her over the wind and landing stargazers.

Dust plumed around them.

"We've taken over the Grotto. This game is over. You have no-where to go. If you bend out of here, I will track you. Archie, it's time to come home. I will explain everything to you. Come home, my sweet boy," Saros said.

Lyra nudged Archie with her elbow, but he was unresponsive. *"Archie! We have to go. Now."* With a firm grip, Lyra pulled on his arm.

He was glued to the spot, refusing to budge. *"My mom."*

The stargazer closest to them lowered a ramp, revealing a woman with long dark hair like Archie's. Lyra noticed how much Archie looked like his mom.

"She's not your mom, remember you said that? Don't believe a word Saros says," Lyra pleaded. She tugged on his arm harder this time.

"Where's your friend, Lyra?" Saros asked, inching forward until she stood on the ground. There was still a good distance between them, but Lyra felt uneasy the closer she got.

Archie remained silent. Lyra gradually guided him towards the Froid. She was afraid to bend if Saros had another trick up her sleeve and could somehow track them.

"You have every right to be angry. Give me a chance to explain. You can decide for yourself after you hear my side," Saros said.

"We have to leave before the dust settles. I don't think my family or dad are with her. This is a trap, Archie. Let's go."

"I awakened your dad only hours ago. We can be Walkers together, Archie. Don't you want to be a family again?"

"You awakened him? How could you?" Archie yelled. His voice washed away with the wind, but he held his chin high and flexed his fingers before squeezing Lyra's hand.

Lyra watched his nostrils flare, then she saw a faint gray glow outlining his body. She leaned into Archie as her head throbbed and she felt dizzy.

"We need to get out of here," Lyra said.

"Can you run?"

"I think so."

Archie pulled her forward and before she knew it, they were running as fast as they could towards the Froid.

Behind them, Saros yelled, "Stop them!"

"Use one of your photons," Archie yelled in her mind.

The moment she pulled a photon out of the bracelet, she felt her feet move faster and her headache immediately wash away.

~Chapter 28~

"Shield," Archie yelled.

Remembering she had the protection skill; Lyra threw a protective bubble around them. Warmth from their breath mixed with the extreme cold caused a thin sheet of frost to crystallize, blocking their view.

Lyra gasped. *"This is the coolest thing I've ever seen."* She reached out to touch the frost.

"It has to be below freezing here. We aren't far enough into the Froid and we need to see. Drop your shield."

Lyra knew he was right and dropped the shield, causing the bubble to burst. Small fragments of frost gracefully fell to the ground.

"I doubt they'll follow us in here, but we need a plan. Even with these suits, it's freezing. We can't stay long. Any ideas?"

"None," Lyra admitted.

The Froid was bathed in a soft, dim glow from Alora's full moons. It didn't look much different from the rest of the planet except for the ice on the ground and covering the boulders. She wondered what kind of creatures could survive such harsh conditions.

"We need to keep moving to keep us warm. We can use the boulders to hide, going from one to another." Archie kept a slow, steady pace as they made their way deeper into the Froid. A heavy wind pushed against them, slowing their pace.

Suddenly, a thunderous roar rattled the ground, knocking them off balance.

"*Not again,*" Lyra shivered.

The bellow grew louder. Lyra steadied herself by grabbing onto Archie's arm.

"We *need to hide,*" Archie said.

Lyra and Archie lowered themselves at the base of the nearest boulder. It was too dark to see more than a few feet in front of them. Despite the light from the full moons, it wasn't enough.

"*Use your mental energy to adjust your vision to the darkness. It helps. Breathe,*" Archie said.

Lyra calmed her breath, returning her heart rate to normal, only to be startled by the presence of two intense greenish eyes glaring directly at them, causing her heart to race again. The massive creature was crouched down like a cat ready to pounce.

With a flick of her wrist, Lyra threw a shield around them. "*Retain your oxygen like we learned to do on the stargazer, and the crystals won't form on the bubble.*"

As the creature advanced, its glowing eyes became narrower, exposing more of its distinctive traits. Along its back, there were bioluminescent spikes that looked like small stars. Starting at the base of its head, they traced their path all the way to the tip of its tail. Iridescent scales covered its neck and body. Curiously, the massive reptilian head tilted and moved closer to them, but then stopped.

The creature shook its head and transformed its scales into bright neon colors, creating distinct patterns on its body and face. Its eyes glowed even more intensely with the brilliant orange outline around them.

With each passing moment, it grew taller and taller until it was upright on its hind legs. Lyra held her breath, waiting for it to attack but it didn't. Instead, it unleashed a thunderous roar that resonated in the air.

"*Don't move,*" Archie warned.

"*Not moving. But I'm not the one it can see.*" As Lyra said those words, she had a strange feeling that the creature saw beyond her invisibility.

Seeing the creature's exposed underbelly, Lyra saw where the scales stopped and a softer looking snake-like skin started. Everything about it looked like the dragons she had seen in movies. She immediately wondered if it could breathe fire.

Then it stretched its wings out. They were greater in width and height than the creature's entire body. With one powerful flap, the creature generated a forceful gust of air that sent them flying about fifty feet away. Lyra was grateful for being able to hold the bubble around them, stopping them from smashing into a boulder. They bounced off a few boulders like a pinball machine before rolling to a stop.

Before she could stand, Archie was already up and screaming at the creature. "We are hiding from danger. Not looking to cause any." He raised his hand, displaying submission.

In one fluid motion, the creature tucked its wings neatly against its body and looked towards the sky. It inhaled deeply through its nostrils.

"Danger?" a deep raspy voice filled Lyra's mind. She stole a quick glance at Archie, wondering if he heard it, too.

"You can talk?" Archie asked. He moved his weight from foot to foot, with his hands loosely hanging by his sides.

"Only to minds like yours and hers." Steam billowed out of his nose, answering Lyra's question about being able to breath fire. *"Your invisibility does you no good here. You can mind talk to me. I've been listening to your conversation since you arrived."*

"Will you harm us?" Lyra asked. She let go of her invisibility, but kept the shield in place.

"If I meant you any harm, you wouldn't be standing there."

"What's your name?" Archie asked.

"You can call me—" the creature made a series of guttural sounds.

"Braken?" Lyra asked, hoping she heard it right.

The creature made another string of throaty sounds, almost like he was laughing. *"You are unlike the other Walkers who dare to step foot in this place. Your strange energy intrigued me, so I had to see for myself. Why are you here? What danger do you speak of?"* Braken asked.

"Saros is here. She's here to finish what Alectryon started. We had no choice but to run into the Froid to avoid being captured by her," Archie said.

Lyra looked at Archie. He nodded as if reading her mind without saying anything. She dropped her shield and they stepped closer, holding hands in case they had to quickly bend away.

Braken laughed again, lowering himself to the ground. He was so close when he spoke that Lyra felt the warmth of his breath. *"Yes, yes, that smell is familiar. But you, boy, you smell of her."*

"She is nothing to me. She is a liar. Do you know how to defeat her?" Archie asked.

"You are her blood. That makes her something to you," Braken sneered. *"You have one thing right. She is a liar. A dangerous one. If she is trying to finish what her father started, she's not just collecting skills from Walkers. She will try to make all magical creatures fight for her. Dragons are much harder to trap. Unlike most creatures, we can bend. I cannot tell you how to defeat her. You are not to be trusted if you are hers. How do I know this isn't a trap?"*

"She's nothing to me. She is holding my dad and Lyra's family captive. We want them back. Galena is planning to trade herself in exchange for Lyra's mom and sister any moment now. Can you help us?" Archie begged.

"Why should I? This is not my battle." Braken shook his body vigorously, like a dog shaking water off after a bath. The vibrant colors and patterns faded to a muted glow.

"Why? Well, if what you say is true, once Galena is gone, who will stop Saros from coming here to capture your kind again? I know your treaty is with Galena only." Archie pointed out.

"*You make a good point, smelly one. Hop on.*" Braken stretched out his arm and lowered his shoulder towards the ground. "*We will gather the others. Quickly, climb on. I'm incredibly ticklish and you don't want me to burst into laughter while you attempt to hold on.*"

Lyra looked at Archie, shrugging her shoulders.

"*How did you suddenly change from not trusting us to let's go gather the others?*" Archie asked, standing firmly where he was.

"*I said I don't trust you. Her, I trust. Humans make everything so complicated. I asked you a question, you gave an excellent answer. Now we do something about it. Start climbing. We can't let Galena sacrifice herself.*"

Lyra walked towards Braken, but stopped when she noticed that Archie wasn't following.

"*What's the plan?*" Archie asked with his arms crossed.

"*You are Walkers, protectors of galaxies and defenders of all beings and creatures within the universe, are you not?*" Braken growled.

"*We aren't trained,*" Lyra said.

"*I can feel how powerful you both are. It's forbidden for her to be here. We must show Saros that she's not welcome. I promise not to hurt anyone unless it's absolutely necessary.*"

Braken made a small shift, causing his entire body to shiver. A bright neon pattern started at the bottom of his paws and ran up to his shoulder, like a path he wanted them to take.

Lyra gasped, "*That's incredible.*"

"Galena gave her permission to be here," Archie said.

"Galena cannot override the deal my kind made with Saros. She didn't ask our permission to be that close to the Froid. We have every right to challenge her. I will protect you both, but be on guard," Braken said as he let out steam through his nostrils, causing dirt and dust to swirl.

Lyra quickly threw a shield around herself until the dust settled. She burst into laughter when she saw Archie covered in a sand-colored dust.

"Funny," Archie said as he brushed the dust from his clothes.

"We don't have a better plan. We need help. Please come with us. It's not every day that we get to ride on the back of a dragon," Lyra said.

"Okay, let's go see Saros." Archie sighed.

"Quickly now. Start climbing," Braken demanded.

Lyra gave herself a little starting room to run and jump onto Braken's massive paw. She pulled herself up, making sure to only step on the brightly lit path of neon colors. Once she got to the end, she sat on the back of his neck as if on a horse. Moments later, Archie lowered himself behind her. She felt his body trembling in fear. He asked if it would be okay to reach around her and hold on to her waist. She nodded in agreement, then leaned forward to hold tight to a spike in front of her.

"Ready," Lyra said.

"Perfect. Now, we talk with the other dragons." Braken lifted his head, his nostrils flaring as he

released a thunderous roar, summoning the other dragons.

~Chapter 29~

Lyra and Archie remained silent when Braken spoke with the other dragons. Lyra wasn't sure if it was a skill that Braken had, but she and Archie couldn't understand what they were saying. No matter how hard she tried, she couldn't make sense of sounds they were making.

Lyra quickly understood why Braken had them sit on the back of his neck. The dragons were animated during the discussion, stomping their feet and thrashing their tails.

After only minutes of this display, Braken spoke to them. *"It has been decided. We will join you on one condition. You both will bend to safety the moment I say so. Agreed?"*

"That was fast," Archie replied.

"Like I said, humans make things harder than they have to be. Do you agree with the terms?"

Lyra and Archie both agreed.

Braken, shining the brightest, led the dragons towards the border. Lyra now understood why it was called a thunder of dragons. They were not stealthy and quiet, but loud and destructive as their tails cracked boulders to pieces along the way.

"Why do we need to bend away when you say? Where would we go?" Lyra asked.

"You both give off pure white energy. None of us have ever seen that before, but we've heard of it. It's the only reason the others agreed to help. Saros must know and we will not let her have that kind of power. Bend to

Earth and find another Walker. They will know what to do," Braken said. *"Lyra, go invisible and stay invisible."*

Lyra's head was filled with questions. She knew it wasn't the right time to ask and there was no way Braken would answer anything right before battle. She set the questions aside and prioritized escaping capture.

The dragons covered a greater distance in less time than she and Archie could on foot. The edge of the Froid quickly came into view. Braken was some distance away and made a series of clicking sounds.

Lyra was amazed by the number of dragons that had joined them. Her fears slowly melted away as she took in the sight. Dragons of different sizes, colors, and types came to defend Alora.

To defend them.

Once they were in formation, Braken walked on with his head held high, hiding Lyra and Archie from view.

The first thing Lyra noticed was how many more stargazers had joined with Saros since they ran into the Froid. This was clearly an attack. Lyra suspected that Saros had no plans to negotiate her mother and sister's release, but this was more than that—it was a full-blown war.

It made sense why Saros wanted to land near the Froid. It was a wide-open space that many wouldn't dare to come.

Saros' stargazer was at the center, protected by a ring of smaller stargazers. The smaller stargazers were so close together that they formed an impenetrable barrier. All the ramps lowered and thousands and thousands of Saros' soldiers stood at attention.

"Braken, we can't win against this many Walkers," Lyra warned.

"They are not all Walkers. The universe will not allow for that many to be awakened at the same time. The universe demands balance. It is why you and Archie have pure energy to balance the power Saros took for herself. If she's smart, she will call it off and retreat once she sees how many dragons have joined," Braken said. *"Remain quiet and invisible, Lyra. Archie and I will do all the talking."*

Braken came to a halt, now positioned outside the Froid, easily seen by the soldiers of Saros. Even though their whispers gave away their surprise, Lyra admired their ability to stay in formation. She just hoped the soldiers weren't as skilled as they were obedient.

Braken rose up on his hind legs and released a warning that shook the ground. Whether or not Saros was aware of them previously, she was certainly aware of them now.

"What makes you think they aren't all awakened?" Archie asked.

"She cannot awaken that many and survive. She cannot teach others to awaken minds, either. It's like a skill, but each awakened mind takes a toll on a Walker that cannot be replenished. Plus, their energy would feel different if they were awakened. There are a few among the groups, but not as many as you think." Braken

made a few other sounds, signaling something to a group of dragons on his right.

The group of dragons nodded in unison, acknowledging their understanding. Lyra watched in awe as they disappeared, leaving a cloud of shimmer behind only for a second. Within seconds that same group of dragons reappeared on top of a few stargazers. They all stood on their hind legs and roared causing the stargazers under them to wobble.

For a brief moment, some of the soldiers broke formation. They quickly regained control of themselves and got back into position.

"They have a skilled manipulator. Someone is controlling their movements. It does not work on awakened minds. Do not worry." Braken advanced.

A different group of dragons launched into the sky only to land in front of Braken, forming a protective barrier between them and Saros' army.

Lyra turned when a dragon with feathers and chicken-like feet bellowed strange sounds. She understood what it said and quickly translated for Archie. *"The dragons in the Blaze are ready and can be here quickly if needed."*

Braken stopped just a few feet away from the frontline of soldiers. He towered over them, casting them in shadow. They moved in unison and changed their position to face him directly. The entire army craned their necks upward. Lyra saw fear etched on their faces and wondered why they hadn't run away. There was no doubt that the manipulator was the one keeping them there against their will. She felt sorry for them. There had to be a way to save her family while sparing their lives.

"I have only been able to communicate with one other Walker before meeting you two. We will use it to our advantage. Archie, you will repeat what I say to Saros. Lyra, stay invisible and do not bring attention to yourself. The leader of the fire-breathing dragons is ready, but I don't want to call on them unless we have to," Braken said.

"You can't breathe fire?" Lyra asked.

"Ice and smoke. No fire. It's time." Braken let out a mighty roar. A warning before he lowered his head to bring Archie into view.

"What do I say?" Archie asked.

"We'll make our terms clear, and if she does not agree with them, we attack. Keep your body language relaxed and composed. It's normal to be afraid, but showing it would only play into her hands. Repeat my words as if they are your own," Braken said.

Lyra watched Saros, who was standing at the edge of the lowered stargazer ramp. She did not look surprised to see Archie. Her arms hung loosely by her sides, with a slight furrowed brow and clenched jaw. She looked annoyed and that made Lyra smile.

Saros lifted her hands, joining them together before parting them. In response, the soldiers cleared a path in the middle wide enough for Braken to go through. She gave a nod to Braken, prompting him to approach her.

As Braken approached, Saros motioned for the soldiers behind him to once again close in, creating a divide between him and the remaining dragons. The ground shook as the other dragons roared angrily and snapped their teeth at the soldiers.

Braken turned towards the dragons and let out a thunderous roar and clicking sounds. Lyra and Archie tightly clung to one of Braken's spikes to prevent themselves from being knocked off.

The dragons obeyed the order and encircled the soldiers, snapping at them but refraining from physical contact. Lyra knew all of this was a demonstration of power from both Saros and the dragons.

"King of Ice Dragons." Saros' voice was somehow amplified without her having to yell. "How *interesting* to see you. Although no one invited you." She scowled.

They were interrupted by another deafening roar.

"The Queen of Fire Dragons is here," Lyra translated for Archie.

"She was supposed to wait for my signal. She never listens." Braken made a sound that Lyra thought was close to a sigh. *"Archie, stand and bow to Ember, the Queen of the Blaze. This will show Saros she is not important and must wait,"* Braken said, lowering his head towards Ember.

Archie rose to his feet and bent forward into a respectful bow. Lyra stayed seated, but lowered her head in a show of respect in case Ember could see through her invisibility.

All of the dragons showed their respect by lowering their heads.

Saros did not bow, instead she looked more annoyed than before. She gave the same signal to clear a passage for Ember.

Ember held her head high and gracefully made her way towards Saros, only stopping when she was next to Braken, giving a quick wink towards her and Archie.

"She's your sister," Lyra said to Braken.

Ember's head bobbed a little, like she was trying to hold in her laughter.

"Yes, my younger sister. Okay, Archie, tell Saros she is not welcome here." Braken demanded, sounding irritated. Lyra was all too familiar with that feeling since her younger sister had a way of getting under her skin.

Archie remained standing and yelled, "You are not welcome here, Saros."

"I see," Saros replied, tilting her head to the side and smiled. "I will not talk to you through my son, King of Ice Dragons. This has nothing to do with you."

"It has everything to do with me. You broke our deal," Archie said, repeating Braken's words. "You will leave now or be forced to leave. The choice is yours."

"It's unlike you, my son, to be someone's pawn. Speak to me with *your* words," Saros dared.

"I am no one's pawn," Archie responded, but quickly stopped when Braken growled. "If war is what you want, war is what you'll have." Archie gasped, cupping his hands over his mouth as if he didn't believe what he just said.

Lyra looked around. The other dragons were nodding in agreement. They were making a low throaty sound. This was not the way she had hoped the meeting would go. She was sure Archie was thinking the same. There had to be another way.

"If war is what you want, then you've already lost. Did you forget I have Lyra's family? Did you forget about your father, my son? Let me tell you a little secret. This," Saros waved her hands about. "All of this is a distraction." Saros snapped her fingers.

Lyra gasped as a soldier dragged Nebula down the ramp, trailed by more soldiers. She had a collar around her neck and some weird harness thing around her torso. It looked like her hands were bound behind her. The soldier tugged on rope-like fibers, pulling her closer to Saros. When they stopped, Nebula fell to her knees, hanging her head low.

Lyra felt her stomach muscles tighten. She wasn't sure if she could keep from vomiting all over the back of Braken's neck. This wasn't how the meeting was supposed to go. She couldn't believe how foolish she was for not recognizing this as a trap. Saros had consistently outsmarted them the whole time.

"I know Lyra is here. Show yourself or I will destroy Nebula right now, in front of you and steal her skill," Saros demanded.

Nebula cried out when a soldier pulled her head back, forcing her to look up at Saros.

"You have 10 seconds to decide or her death is on your hands," Saros said.

Just then, Lyra saw something out of the corner of her eye. There was movement near the ramp to Saros' stargazer. *"Don't look, but I saw someone bend near Saros' ramp."*

"Finally, they're here. We need to keep Saros distracted. It's time to show yourself," Braken said.

"You knew?" Lyra and Archie said at the same time.

"Yes, I'll explain later. Show yourself now, Lyra," Braken demanded.

Lyra dropped her invisibly. "I'm here."

"Lyra, dear Lyra. I hoped you were. I mean, I thought you'd try to do something idiotic, like sneak on my stargazer and play hero. But I know you're never far from my son."

"You can't win," Archie said.

"You think you can control the universe with fear and power? You think stealing skills will make you powerful enough to rule the universe? It won't. You're weak," Lyra said.

"Careful, Lyra," Braken growled.

"What are you doing?" Archie asked.

"Oh, you sweet naïve children. I've already won. I have Nebula. You were the real distraction." She smiled. "Archie, I will be back for you. Give it time and you'll see. You will choose to join me when you understand that this is the way things should be." Saros signaled to her soldiers to drag Nebula back inside the stargazer.

"No!" Lyra yelled. She reached her hands forward, but nothing happened.

"Let her go," Braken said.

Braken's words were drowned out by the deafening roars all around them and the intense ground shaking.

Lyra remained motionless; her eyes fixed on Saros as she followed the soldiers who were dragging Nebula further into the stargazer. Then the ramp lifted and the stargazer vanished.

Oddly, the other stargazers and all the soldiers who were left behind started flickering.

"Holograms," Archie yelled. "She tricked us with holograms."

"Look," Braken said. *"I see something."*

As the clouds of dirt and dust settled, Lyra squinted, struggling to understand what she was seeing.

"It's just another trick," Lyra said.

But she couldn't look away as her mom, dad, and sister slowly came into view. They looked thinner and were completely covered in dirt. A few feet behind them, Castor came into view, supporting Pollux. Then Blue and Nebula walked hand-in-hand with smiles on their faces.

"How?" Lyra wasn't sure if she'd said it or thought it, but she couldn't believe what she was seeing.

"Are they really here?" Lyra asked Braken.

"They are, little one. Go to them," a female voice filled her head and she knew immediately that it was Ember.

Braken lowered his head, but Lyra couldn't wait. She vanished only to reappear a few feet in front of her family. She took in the scene. The last bit of dust settled, letting her see her parents and sister for the first time in what felt like forever.

Right behind them, she noticed Helix, who was supporting Archie's dad. He was in a worse condition than the others. Even so, he nodded towards her. She smiled back then ran the rest of the way to her family.

They silently hugged for what felt like forever before anyone moved.

"How?" Lyra asked.

"We were all a part of Galena's plan. You and Archie were the real distraction so the others could sneak aboard Saros' ship to rescue everyone," Braken admitted. *"Archie, go to your dad. He needs your help. We will speak soon. We have much to discuss, Universe Walkers."* Braken winked at Lyra and as soon as Archie's feet hit the ground all the dragons vanished except for Ember, the Queen of the Fire Dragons.

"You are safe for now, young Walkers. Saros will return. When you meet with Braken, I will be there and will properly introduce myself. Until then, train every day. Saros won't give up. I'm afraid this is only the beginning," Ember said.

Lyra and Archie nodded their understanding then bowed low. When they stood, Ember was gone.

Lyra wiped her tears away with her sleeve. She couldn't believe that she had her family back, all of them. She hugged them again, not wanting to ever let them go.

"Ouch," Nova said.

"Oh, sorry." Lyra slightly loosened her grip. "I don't ever want to let go of you guys."

Lyra and her family spoke for a short time before Galena materialized near them. She had no idea if Archie had talked with his dad, but they stood waiting for Galena to say something as well.

"We shouldn't stay out here for long," Galena said. "We have beds set up at the Grotto. Nebula has plenty of tonics. She will tend to your wounds."

Lyra let go of her family and walked a few steps closer towards Galena. "Thank you for saving my family and Archie's dad. I'm sorry for not trusting your plan. We thought you were going to give yourself to Saros and knew she wouldn't give our families back."

Archie joined her. "Thank you."

"I'm sorry I misled you both and I hope you will forgive me. I needed you to get to the dragons. We can't speak to them directly, but we have a way to communicate through hand signals and now we have a way to speak with them directly. I never thought I would be so lucky to meet a Universe Walker and here the two of you stand. Let's get to the Grotto. Everyone needs water, food, a good washing and a long rest. Then we will celebrate today's victory."

"Universe Walker, that's what Braken called us," Archie said.

"So, that's his name. Yes, it explains why you guys have so many skills. I'll explain more when we get back. See you there," Galena said, then vanished, leaving a faint shimmer behind.

~Chapter 30~

During the time spent on Alora, which was only about a week on Earth, everyone's cuts and bruises magically disappeared thanks to Nebula's healing skill and a massive amount of tonics she made everyone drink.

Lyra's parents said that they had never felt better and wished they could take Nebula back to Earth with them.

It took Mr. Seren a little longer to heal than the others. His color slowly returned and he smiled more than Lyra had ever seen.

Even though Lyra's parents and Mr. Seren understood what a Walker was, they had a hard time accepting that Lyra and Archie could travel through the fabrics of the cosmos at the speed of thought. They had a harder time coming to terms with dragons and other mythological creatures being real. On the other hand, Nova wouldn't stop telling everyone that she had been right all along and knew unicorns existed.

Nova was convinced that Lyra was a witch with magical powers and couldn't be convinced otherwise. She begged Lyra to bend to one side of the room and back again. But her parents asked her not to keeping doing it because watching someone bend made them feel nauseous. They particularly disliked when she went invisible. They came up with some rules, which Lyra didn't mind following.

While the Stewarts were busy catching up on lost time, Archie and his dad had to navigate their healing differently. Archie wasn't physically hurt, but it was a lot to accept that Saros was really his mom. She had deceived them and hurt them.

Mr. Seren apologized every day to Archie for working too much and for not knowing what Saros was capable of doing. He promised Archie that things would change when they returned to Earth. He planned on stepping back from working so much and promised to take Archie camping.

Nebula suggested they consider talking with a counselor. She recommended a Walker, experienced with situations like this, and could visit them on Earth as often as they needed. Talking to an Earth counselor would mean they couldn't talk about Walkers or the actual truth of what happened. It would be hard for anyone on Earth to believe the story of Galaxy Walkers or that Archie's mom had really been a power-hungry rogue Walker looking to reset the universe.

They agreed to speak with the counselor Nebula recommended when they got back to Earth.

During their time of healing on Alora, Galena briefed Lyra and Archie about her elaborate plan. Lyra and Archie meeting Braken was not a coincidence. The fact that he could communicate with them was surprising, but it only made the plan that much easier.

The plan had to be altered when Saros captured Nebula, a development no one had expected. Thanks to Archie's photon bracelet, things turned out well. Using the mental energy boost, Nebula broke free, got help, and they all rescued Lyra's family and Archie's dad without Saros ever realizing she was gone.

When it was time to go back to Earth, Lyra experienced a bittersweet feeling of sadness and happiness. Even though her time on Alora was a mix of good and bad, she felt like she found herself and what she was meant to do. She knew she'd see Galena, Nebula, the twins, Blue, and Helix again.

It was strange returning to Earth. It was like nothing happened and barely any time had passed. No one knew what had truly happened. A skilled Walker altered the Stewart's memories and Lyra's grandparents for their own safety and to keep Walkers a secret.

Lyra and Archie went back to school like usual, trying to ignore the weight of the world that now rested on her shoulders. They would always be Walkers, protectors of the galaxies, of the universe.

Universe Walkers.

Lyra couldn't wait to learn more about what it meant to be a Universe Walker. The twins told them to continue life as usual and soon they would be called back for training. Since time went much slower on Earth, they could bend to Alora for days to train and back to Earth without anyone knowing.

Meanwhile, Archie's father quit his corporate job to focus on spending time with his son. They went shopping for both new clothes and camping equipment. Archie began dressing more appropriately for his age, but his wild hair stayed unchanged. Not only had Archie's appearance changed, but he also gained more confidence in himself. He joined the chess club and even asked Lyra to go with him to the sixth-grade end-of-year dance.

Of course, Lyra said yes. She wouldn't miss experiencing her first dance with her best friend.

Seeing Archie's confidence gave Lyra the boost she needed to ask her parents for help with reading and spelling. They apologized for not noticing it sooner and immediately hired a tutor to help with her studies. Her grades improved to the point where she could join the end-of-year field trip to the zoo.

With everything going well, Lyra couldn't help but feel alone. While her family wasn't allowed to keep their memories of everything that happened, Mr. Seren's memories weren't altered.

Lyra understood it was better for her family this way. If they couldn't remember anything about Walkers, they would continue living their lives normally. She didn't want them to remember the constant fear of being held hostage by Saros. But without them remembering anything, she felt like she had no one to talk to about what happened. It would be a part of her that they would never know and a part of her that she'd always have to keep secret.

Archie's dad needed to remember in case Saros came back for him. He needed to be prepared in case Saros tried to trick him into thinking his wife was returning home. As much as Lyra knew this was best for all, she couldn't help but feel a little jealous that Archie got to talk to his dad about everything.

A few months passed before the twins visited Lyra and Archie. They told them that they would bend to Alora every weekend for training. Since time occurred differently on Earth than on Alora, no one would ever find out.

The first time they returned to Alora, Galena updated them on Saros recent activity and it was very upsetting. She was going from galaxy to galaxy awakening random minds. If someone had a skill she didn't want, she left them. For the skills she wanted, she would steal the skill, destroying the person. It was only a matter of time before she got all the skills she wanted and would become the strongest Walker of all time.

"She's trying to become a Universe Walker," Archie said.

"Exactly. We're mostly concerned about the damage she'll do before the power becomes too much and she destroys herself," Helix said.

"Will we destroy ourselves?" Lyra asked.

"Only if you try to use all of your skills at once and burn out. To get ultimate power, we expect Saros to do just that."

"If Lyra and I are Universe Walkers, can't we stop her?" Archie asked.

"We sure hope so, but we need to train you harder than ever. Are you ready for the challenge?" Galena asked.

Lyra and Archie nodded in agreement.

The newly awakened minds that Saros left behind were brought to training planets, including Alora. Every time Lyra and Archie returned for training, they were introduced to someone newly awakened.

Strangely, the new Walkers were oddly manifesting multiple skills, like Lyra and Archie had. Lyra wanted to ask Galena about it, but she wasn't around often. They were told that she was busy meeting with other rulers, trying to come up with a plan to stop Saros.

One training session, Lyra and Archie asked Helix about the new Walkers. He said, "The universe is a living thing, constantly growing and adapting. Every time Saros steals a new skill or awakens a mind and brings them to her side, the universe responds. It's a delicate balance. We need to stop Saros before she becomes too powerful. She will destroy every planet and lifeform when she feels she's powerful enough to do so. Alectryon wanted to reset the universe once, too and we were able to stop him."

"Why can't we stop Saros now?" Archie asked.

"We don't have enough experienced or trained Universe Walkers. Unfortunately, Saros is ahead of us. But we will be ready when it's time. I believe we can stop her." Helix handed Archie and Lyra a new wrist band. "Keep these on. They are new lifelines that can go further and faster, thanks to Archie's photon bracelet invention. Saros doesn't have access to the photon bracelets. I think those make up for the loss of time we've had to train."

"It's not right what she's doing and we can't do anything to stop her right now," Lyra said as she clasped the new bracelet behind the one Archie made for her. One day, her parents asked where the other one went. Archie told them that she was so upset when it broke in P.E. class so, he made her a new one. They loved the story.

"We have hundreds of skilled Walkers stationed all over, which has slowed Saros down a bit. The twins are waiting for you in the training arena." Helix smiled.

Lyra and Archie nodded, then materialized outside of the arch.

"Wait," Archie said. "I have a plan. Are you game?"

Lyra held her hand out for him to take. "I'm always up for an adventure."

ABOUT THE AUTHOR

Kris Paulsen is a passionate writer and avid reader who finds joy in crafting stories that transport readers to new worlds. When she's not reading or writing, she enjoys spending quality time with her family and crafting. She currently lives on the West Coast with her amazing husband, three kids, and two dogs.

ACKNOWLEDGEMENTS

I want to express my gratitude to my family for their love and support. They cheered me on every step of the way and shared in my joy when I reached the finish line.

A big thank you to all of my readers. If it weren't for you, this book would be collecting dust on my shelf.

This wouldn't have been possible without a fantastic team. Special thanks to Kim Chance, my developmental editor. A big thank you to the multiple proofreaders, beta readers, and line editors. This book owes its success to the incredible team behind it.

TO MY READERS

Thank you for joining Lyra and Archie on their adventure! If you enjoyed reading GALAXY WALKERS, please leave a review and share your experience. Each review truly matters! I appreciate your support!

www.ingramcontent.com/pod-product-compliance
Lightning Source LLC
Chambersburg PA
CBHW022120310726
48972CB00007B/2116